"ARE YOU MAD BECAUSE I DIDN'T LET YOU FINISH WHAT YOU STARTED?"

Doug grabbed her arms. "Lady, if I'd been that determined to make love to you, nothing would have stopped me. And by the way, I don't remember an awful lot of resistance from you."

Marti tried to wrench free. "You're too persistent. You don't even hear the word *no.*"

"I didn't hear it because you didn't say it! You want me whether you'll admit it or not. Just like I want you."

With a great effort, she shook free of him. "But I don't want a one-night stand. I can't live with that. And you can't offer me anything else."

CANDLELIGHT ECSTASY CLASSIC ROMANCES

CANDLELIGHT ECSTASY ROMANCES®

HEAD OVER HEELS

Terri Herrington

A CANDLELIGHT ECSTASY ROMANCE®

Published by
Dell Publishing Co., Inc.
1 Dag Hammarskjold Plaza
New York, New York 10017

ISBN: 0-440-13489-7

Printed in the United States of America

October 1986

10 9 8 7 6 5 4 3 2 1

WFH

For Gina, the survivor, who sees beginnings where others see endings. This one's for you.

Special thanks to J. Y. Recording in West Monroe, Louisiana, for spending valuable time teaching me about the studio and the life of a recording engineer.

To Our Readers:

We have been delighted with your enthusiastic response to Candlelight Ecstasy Romances®, and we thank you for the interest you have shown in this exciting series.

In the upcoming months we will continue to present the distinctive sensuous love stories you have come to expect only from Ecstasy. We look forward to bringing you many more books from your favorite authors and also the very finest work from new authors of contemporary romantic fiction.

As always, we are striving to present the unique, absorbing love stories that you enjoy most—books that are more than ordinary romance. Your suggestions and comments are always welcome. Please write to us at the address below.

Sincerely,

The Editors
Candlelight Romances
1 Dag Hammarskjold Plaza
New York, New York 10017

HEAD OVER HEELS

CHAPTER ONE

Marti Jackson felt the strangling grip of panic as she struggled to stay attached to the skis whisking her down the steep Breckenridge slopes. All control had vanished when her speed took over, hurling her toward a bumpy stretch of ice just before the drop-off to the black expert trail, Sizzler. Icy wind whistled in her ears and stung her face, and unable to do anything else, Marti screamed.

A wayward limb slapped one pole from her hand, and the other flew like a misguided spear to some distant target. As if a part of the mad production, a well-planted mogul loomed up in front of her, snapping the skis off her boots and sending her into a flip that dropped her on a headfirst slide. Desperately, vainly, she clutched at powder and ice for something to stop her descent.

Pain tore down her left side and shot through her head while she tumbled down the expert slope, snow packing into her mouth and goggles, jagged edges of mountain ripping her clothes as she fell. From the corner of her eye she saw trees, bushes, rocks, each threatening their own punishment if she ventured too close, but her wild momentum gave her no choice in direction. Another scream that sounded small and far away grated from her throat, and she felt her leg being snagged by a thorny bush, the whirl of her body as it protested the sudden stop, a sharp pain through her head . . .

And then nothing.

"She's hurt! Call the Ski Patrol!"

Through the haze of dizziness she heard the voice, deep and urgent, shouting to nameless, faceless people, breaking through her blackness and drawing her back to the blinding light. Looking up through her icy goggles, she could barely make out the imposing figure in black bent over her. His eyes were hidden behind mirrored glasses, and his black mustache and dark hair made him seem sinister.

Clicking out of his skis, he knelt beside her and slid off her frosted goggles, muttering a whispered "Damn!" at the blood trickling down her temple. "You all right?" he asked in a clear, soft voice that made her feel less alone.

She didn't answer at first, only looked up at him, rounding her blue eyes for focus. Her blond hair was matted with ice and tangled wildly around her arms, and her full lips quivered at the corners as she blinked back the well of tears glossing her eyes. "I . . . I don't think so," she whispered.

The man dropped his glasses, letting them hang from the band around his neck. His eyes, framed in thick black lashes and reddened from the dry cold, were warm, comforting, and the color of summer grass. Summer grass, she thought mournfully. Like the Florida grass that grew back home where tempera-

tures were not deadly, where nature was soft and predictable, where a fall from a pair of skis meant a
splash in the ocean. His soft eyes came closer, study-
ing the dilation of her pupils. A gloved hand reached
out to touch her face, but instinctively she recoiled
and tried to sit up.

"Don't move," he said, taking her shoulders and
laying her back down. The clouds whirling in her head
forced her to acquiesce. "You almost cashed in on that
last mogul."

"What's a mogul?" she asked mournfully as the first
twist of pain made its way to her consciousness.

"Those little bumps on the run that helped you with
your acrobatics. I've never met a skier who didn't
know what a mogul was."

When she closed her eyes and didn't answer, he set
a comforting hand on her shoulder. "You hit your
head pretty hard, and I wouldn't be surprised if something's broken. Help will be here in a minute."

"You mean I don't have to roll the rest of the way
down the mountain?" she groaned defenselessly.

The man breathed a quiet chuckle. "You gave it a
good try, but I'm afraid you're a hazard. A few others
wiped out trying to get out of your way."

Again she raised up, wincing as she supported herself on her injured wrist. "Anybody hurt?"

The man lowered her back again. "No. The skiers in
this area are pretty good. They're used to dodging
hurling bodies."

"I could have killed someone," she said, clutching
her head. The warm feel of blood on her fingers made
her wonder irrelevantly where she had lost her glove,
then she caught herself and realized the extent of her

injuries. "I could have killed *myself.*" Closing her eyes tightly, she moaned, "I knew I should have taken lessons."

"Lessons?" The stranger's eyes lost their concern and filled with incredulity. "Do you mean to tell me you're a beginner?"

Marti nodded and tried to bend the numb fingers of her left hand.

"If you're a beginner," he said, his voice taking on an impatient edge, "what are you doing up here alone? And how in the hell did you wind up on the expert slope? Are you nuts?"

Ignoring his last question, Marti managed a shrug. "I didn't know I was heading for a black slope. I was trying to follow the beginner greens, but there weren't any."

His emerald eyes still glared at her, leaving her cold and unaccountably ashamed, as if she had somehow disappointed him. "Didn't you study the map?"

The distant hum of an engine distracted her momentarily, and she mumbled, "What map?"

"The trail map!" he shouted. "Don't tell me you didn't get a map!"

"I didn't know about any maps," she snapped.

"Can't ski and don't even have a map," he said, yanking off his glove and slapping it against his thigh. "Do you at least know the difference in green, blue, and black?"

"Yes!" she shouted back. "I'm not entirely stupid! And in case you haven't noticed, I'm suffering at the moment. Can you please flex your vocal cords somewhere else?"

Their eyes held each other in silent battle for a moment, the tension breaking only when he turned his glove inside out and dabbed at the cut along her hairline. "Sorry," he said more quietly, wincing when she winced.

The roaring of the engine grew louder as the snowmobile appeared over the top of Sizzler. New fear and uncertainty welled in Marti's eyes, and the defiant way she bit her lip and glanced toward the vehicle softened his heart. Well, he thought, whatever idiotic thing she had done today, she had paid for it. A lecture on the safety rules of skiing seemed a little redundant at this point.

A tremor softened the compressed lines of her lips, tugging at some protective instinct within him. Immediately he began to unzip his coat. "Cold?" he asked.

The question seemed absurd in light of the fact that she was lying like a Gulf Coast fish preserved in Arctic ice. "I've been cold since I got to Colorado," she muttered. "It serves me right for leaving Florida."

He began to drag his coat off his thick arms, and she reached out to stop him. "Keep it on. I'm tougher than I look."

"I'm sure you are," he said with a slight note of sarcasm. "But you need to stay warm." Gently he draped the big jacket over her, tucking it under her arms to keep the draft out. "I'm Doug Duziak."

"Marti Jackson," she offered as her eyes strayed to the broad shoulders and corded biceps swelling under his tight turtleneck shirt. The instant attraction angered her, for the last thing she needed now was to be interested in a man. He reached out to touch her leg, and she drew back again. "Don't."

"Hold still," he ordered gently, as if her modesty

15

was ill-timed. "I'm just checking to see if anything's broken. Does this hurt?"

Marti sucked in a breath when he twisted her knee. "Of course it hurts. And so does my ankle. Want to . twist it too?" she asked sardonically.

He let her go. "Are you mad at the mountain for besting you or at me for seeing it happen?"

Marti bristled at her transparency. "I'm mad at myself for letting my life turn into a bad circus."

An amused grin transformed his face, deepening the lines that webbed his eyes. "Was this one of your death-defying acts?"

Marti blew out a long, weary sigh that became visible in the cold air. "It wasn't supposed to be. It was supposed to be an exercise in control." A dry, hoarse laugh broke from her throat. "Do you ever feel like the whole world is playing a big joke on you, everyone acting out a role, and that any minute they'll all jump out and say, 'Surprise! We were just kidding! Things aren't really as bad as they seem!' "

A pensive cloud fell over Doug's eyes, and he tilted his head and smiled down at her. "Yeah," he said at length. "I've felt that way a time or two."

Marti looked into his eyes, and for a moment felt a connection between them that she could not explain. Before she could respond, the snowmobile appeared next to her and a man with a leathered face and hair the color of dirty snow jumped out, the white medical cross on his red uniform jacket testifying to his ability as an emergency medical technician. "Hot dogger?" he asked, squatting down next to Marti.

"Worse," Doug said. "A beginner."

The man gave a high laugh. "On Sizzler? You

should have known by the name. We don't name green slopes Sizzler and Psychopath. We name them dull things, like Four O'Clock Run and Lower Lehman. Names that don't call up images of fear and terror in the hearts of pretty little clutzes."

"I'm not a clutz. And it didn't matter what the name of the slope was. I just went where my skis took me."

His grin rankled Marti as much as his merciless hands as strong impersonal fingers probed at her muscles and tested her joints, tilted her face and stretched her eyelids, his face registering amusement with each groan. When he had finished he reached in his sled and pulled out a neck brace. "Until we can get some X-rays we need to keep your neck stable with this. Then we'll put you on this sled and pull you down," he told her. Then, turning to Doug, he asked, "Are you with her?"

"No," Marti cut in quickly, wanting to end her interaction with the stranger as soon as possible. "I was with a friend but I got separated from her."

"I'll get her skis and follow you down," Doug said.

Her protest was cut off when the man put the brace on her, then wrapped her and buckled her onto the coffinlike contraption and lifted her onto the sled. "What if this rolls over?" she asked suspiciously.

"It won't," the man said with an annoying grin. "I do this all day long and it's the safest way to get you down." He started to get in, then turned back to Marti in afterthought. "But if the sled does come loose and you pass me, I'll just meet you at the bottom."

Marti failed to see the humor and glared at Doug, who bit back his smile. The technician started the engine, and she watched Doug snap on his skis and nod to the driver.

Marti closed her eyes as the snowmobile began to move. Desperately, she tried to contain her fear as bumps jarred her and slides shook her. The smell of unmerciful cold laced with exhaust fumes and the sound of the engine pulling her down the mountain that had overcome her made the ordeal seem worse than it was. How could this have happened her first time down? she asked herself with rage.

The snowmobile took a sharp turn, and she swallowed back a wave of nausea. Maybe relocating to Colorado hadn't been such a good idea after all. She had hoped the change of scenery and a new set of people could help her to forget her problems. But she hadn't expected nature to assault her on her first day, leaving her with a whole medical chart full of physical injuries almost as severe as her emotional one.

It seemed as if a week had passed, but the clock showed that only four hours had crept by before her sprained knee, ankle, and wrist were wrapped and her head injury was declared a concussion. "The nearest hospital is in Denver, so we can't keep you overnight for observation as we'd like," the young doctor who looked distressingly like a retired-lifeguard-turned-ski-bum told her.

"Good," Marti said, sitting up. "You've already exposed me to enough radiation to power Manhattan, and nothing's broken. It would be silly to put me in the hospital."

Doug, who had remained with her every step of the way, despite her irritable attempts to make him leave her, leaned on the doorjamb, arms crossed over his chest. "Why would you want to admit her?" he asked.

"There could be complications. Concussions are nothing to fool around with."

"I appreciate your concern," Marti said, determined to head off whatever the doctor was leading up to, "but I feel fine. I'm not even going to miss my first day of work tomorrow."

The tanned doctor stepped forward, his voice firm. "You need to take it easy. If there are complications, they'll occur tonight."

Marti raised her hand to stem the negative possibilities, as if the gesture could ensure her safety. "I don't have time for complications. I'm going to be fine."

"Well, there probably won't be any," the doctor said. "But just in case, you'll have to get someone to stay with you tonight and check you every two hours."

"Check me for what?"

The doctor rolled his eyes heavenward, as if he hadn't encountered such obstinancy in a long while. "That blow to your head may cause some bleeding, and checking the dilation and constriction of your pupils, among other things, is a way to monitor it. Can someone stay with you or not?"

Helplessness overwhelmed her again. "Amanda's the only one I know here, and she works nights."

"You know me," Doug said, a slight grin working at his mouth.

"Then you'll stay with her?" the doctor asked.

"No, he will not," Marti objected. "Until my accident, I had never seen him in my life. He's been very helpful today, but I can't spend the night with a total stranger."

"We could helicopter you to Denver and admit you to the hospital," Doug pointed out as though it would be his decision. The beguiling smile widening across his face told her he was enjoying her dilemma.

Marti felt the heat of uncertainty flushing her face. She had come here to get over one man, and now she was tangled up with another who was obviously taking full advantage of a situation in which she had little control. But her choices were slim, she told herself. Glancing at Doug, she bit her cheek. Perhaps he was enjoying it so much because he knew she would refuse. How many complete strangers would actually spend an entire night caring for someone who had been moody and rude to him all day?

It didn't matter, she thought finally. All she had to do was convince the doctor she had good intentions, and when she was back in her apartment she could do as she pleased. "All right," she said finally, meeting Doug's eyes daringly. "You asked for it."

He took up her challenge with a bright smile. "I sure did."

Apprehension bristled inside her at his unexpected enthusiasm. What if she couldn't get rid of him after they were out of the clinic? What if his determination to stay was stronger than her determination for him to leave? Well, she told herself. She may be injured, but her experiences with men had at least taught her self-protection. Regardless of what he had in mind, Marti could take care of herself.

When they had both been armed, Marti with a crutch and Doug with an instruction sheet on how to

20

care for her, they made their way out of the clinic and stood facing each other in the glaring sunshine. Marti's head felt as if it had served as replacement for a boxer's punching bag, and she narrowed her eyes against the harsh light.

"Head hurt?" he asked.

"Do pigs get sunburned?"

He laughed and considered it a moment. "I don't know."

"They do," she assured him. "Believe me."

Doug smiled appreciatively at her, taking advantage of her seeming lack of defenses to study her for a moment. It was the first time he had seen her standing at close range, and her five feet five inches surprised him since she had looked so tiny on the mountain. Her scrapes and bruises, and the weary way she leaned on her crutch, made her look incredibly vulnerable, and he suspected that the strength, independence, and stubbornness he had witnessed were her means of self-protection. Pain gnawed at her face, touching something new inside of Doug, something that made him uncomfortable. He pulled his sunglasses out of his pocket and slid them over her ears.

"Thanks," she said, unable to reject that small bit of relief.

Doug glanced down at the sheet he had been given. "Says here that you can't take anything except aspirin. They don't want you masking any symptoms." He threw her an apologetic glance. "Wish there was something I could do."

"Just help me get to the shuttle bus," she said, realizing that she would have to lean on him just long enough to get home. What she wanted more than anything was to lie down and forget the day had happened. "I'm staying at—"

"The Unicorn," he finished for her, a twinkle in his eyes. "I saw you there yesterday."

"Oh?" she asked warily. "Are you staying there too?"

"I live there. Across the parking lot from you."

Doug watched the pain on her face mingle with intense suspicion, and he wondered why that simple fact could upset her. He remembered seeing her drive up in the parking lot, remembered the familiar spark that had sizzled inside him at the flowing mane of hair, the bright, defiant eyes, the perfect figure, the body that declared its confidence to the world. It wasn't unusual for him to feel that sort of attraction to a woman, that sort of compelling interest in physical beauty. And when he had seen her leaving on the shuttle for the slopes this morning, he had grabbed his own gear and taken the next bus, hoping to catch up to her and meet her by "accident." He had never counted on finding her in a heap at the bottom of Sizzler or being her rescuer and keeper for the rest of the night. But he certainly didn't mind it.

He cupped her elbow and started to help her walk. "I guess you realize by now that a beginner should never ski alone. What if you hadn't met me to help you?"

She leaned away from his touch. "I would have managed," she insisted. "Besides, I started out with a friend, another woman who works at the Unicorn, but I fell and lost track of her. It's okay, though. I don't really need that much help."

"Right," Doug said, amusement tugging at his lips.

22

"Somehow I get the feeling you said that earlier today. Possibly when someone urged you to take lessons?"

The truth of his observation forced a grin to break through her frown. "She didn't urge hard enough."

"Still part of the conspiracy?" he asked.

"I'm sure of it," she said, but the amusement drained from her face, and he wished he could see her eyes through the mirrored lenses covering them. "You know," she said as they reached the shuttle bus that made a routine run through town and could be caught at twenty-minute intervals, "in spite of my attitude, I really do appreciate your help today. It's just that I'm used to doing things on my own. I don't like leaning on people."

He turned to face her when they reached the door of the bus. "Why not?"

Because when you lean on someone you deserve to fall, she wanted to say, but instead she simply sighed and said, "That's just the way I am."

"Well, at least give me the benefit of being the way I am," he said. "And I don't like turning my back on a lady in distress."

Conceding defeat for the moment, Marti glanced at the skis in the racks on the outside of the bus. "Do you know where my skis are?"

"In my locker," he said, "and so are your boots. I put them there when I got your shoes for you, but I don't think you'll be needing them for a while."

Marti offered a grin and a slight nod, then stared at the steps, trying to decide just how she would manage them with only one crutch. But before she could take the first step, Doug took her by the waist and lifted her inside. The security of his hands frightened her, and

23

his concern rankled her. She didn't want to need him or be grateful to him. She didn't even want to like him.

Marti decided it was time to finagle her way out of having him stay with her all night, before this selfless attention made her weak. "You know, you really don't have to do all this. Staying with me all day, promising to take care of me all night . . ."

Doug propped his elbow on the back of her seat and leaned toward her, his face inclined in masculine appreciation. "I'm looking forward to it," he said seductively, a hint of amusement twinkling in his jade eyes. "I've always liked playing doctor with beautiful women."

Marti only stared at him in answer, trying to decide if breaking his face was worth the risk of injuring her good hand.

CHAPTER TWO

"I don't think that's funny," Marti said, clipping out each word with bitter emphasis.

Doug breathed a laugh and slipped into the seat behind her. "Hey, it was just a joke."

"You have a distorted sense of humor."

"Well, at least I've got one."

Marti bit her lip and gazed out the window opposite her as the bus began to pull out of its space. They're all creeps, she thought with infuriation. One minute shaking her with gentleness, the next minute hitting on her with a smooth line like he had just delivered under the guise of humor. She couldn't wait to slam the door in his face when she got to her apartment.

"Look, I'm sorry. I was just trying to lighten things up a little. You look so serious."

Marti cast him a disparaging glance. "I *am* serious," she told him. "About a lot of things. Among them bad headaches, sprained ankles, and lecherous men."

"Lecherous men?" he asked on an amazed laugh. "Is that what you think I am?"

"I lump most men in that category when they suggest we 'play doctor.'"

Doug slumped back in his seat, a defeated, disbelieving gleam in his eyes.

"Well, what would *you* call that?" she asked.

"Bad taste," he conceded. "For which I have already apologized."

A moment of silence followed as the bus began heading downhill to their resort. Marti closed her eyes and leaned her head back against the window, reminding herself that she needed to get along with him if they were going to be neighbors.

Why, she wondered, did that bit of information bother her so? Was it that bit of attraction she felt when she looked in his eyes that frightened her so, or the fact that he'd been interested enough to watch and remember her? And why shouldn't it frighten her? He had the same riveting charm that Mike had when she'd first met him.

She breathed a long, deep sigh. He probably even worked at the Unicorn, since most of the employees lived in her section. She knew from past experience that it didn't pay to create hostility with co-workers. "Do you work at the Unicorn?" she asked almost grudgingly.

Doug ran his hand through his tousled black hair and looked out his window as if trying to decide whether to answer. "No," he said. "I'm a recording engineer. My studio's not far from here."

He watched her nod without much interest, then gaze out the windows at the snow-coated spruces and craggy summits rising in the distance behind them. Doug followed her gaze and wondered if she saw the majestic beauty or the overwhelming power of Colorado's version of nature. Fidgeting with his mustache, he glanced back at her, saw the sad sparkle of disillusionment in her blue eyes, and he recognized it, for it was something he knew. A long sigh tore out of him. Maybe he had made a mistake taking her under his wing. What had started out as physical attraction and the human urge to help someone in trouble was fast becoming a royal pain. If she'd only smile more, he thought, but it seemed the longer they knew each other the more she drew herself inward. He couldn't remember the last time a woman had shunned him this way, if one ever had. If he had any sense, he'd do what he'd obligated himself to do, then forget they'd ever met. If only she didn't have eyes that reached inside him, or that long, silky, tangled hair that compelled him to run his fingers through it. Hell, he thought, shaking off the absurd notion. He didn't have time to be distracted by another woman. The one relationship he already had was driving him crazy. Trish still clung to him as if her whole future depended on him, draining him in a way that left him empty and numb. Caring for people meant giving up too much. No, there was no room in his life for another woman who needed him, and yet he couldn't stand the idea of not seeing beyond that guarded facade just once.

The bus passed the sign bearing the white unicorn at the peak of a snow-covered mountain, and he leaned up to her seat. "A lot's happened since you last saw that sign, huh?" he asked in a voice more understanding than she wanted to acknowledge.

Marti shrugged. "Just another day at the circus." Gravely, she glanced back at him, forcing a smile. "You know, I do have a personality under here. I just

27

need to get around the self-pity before I can find it again."

"I know," he said softly. "I've been seeing little peeks of it all day long. The worst thing is that you keep looking at me as the enemy." Marti wished she could tell him it wasn't true. But it was true, and she didn't think it was wise to convince herself otherwise.

He stood up when the bus stopped, held out a hand for her to lean on as she situated her crutch. He helped her off the bus, steadied her when she reached the ice. "So where to?" he asked. "Your place or mine?"

"Both," Marti said carefully. "You go to your place, I'll go to mine."

Doug stopped mid-stride and watched, amazed, as Marti started to make her way across the ice to "employees' row." "Wait a minute," he said. "I told the doctor I'd stay with you."

Marti reached the steps leading to her apartment. "I don't need a baby-sitter. I'm fine. I just want to lie down."

Her easy dismissal of him made him more determined not to leave her. "And who's going to wake you up every two hours to check your pupils?"

"I have an alarm clock and a mirror," she said, negotiating the first step as he followed up behind her.

"Oh?" he blared. "And what if complications arise? What if you should get a hematoma? An alarm clock won't wake you up, and all the self-reliance in the world won't help."

"I'll chance it," she said.

"Like you chanced skiing without a trail map or lessons?"

"I'll be fine!" she said again, but as her foot hit the

last step it slipped out from under her. Dropping her crutch, she fell backward into Doug's arms.

"My place or yours?" he asked down at her, the gentle "I told you so" in his tone breaking her fragile constitution.

"I told you." Her voice broke, and tears sprang to her eyes, and she widened them to keep them from spilling.

"And I told you," he said, his timbre softening at the sudden flash of vulnerability. "You're stuck with me until tomorrow."

Without warning he slipped an arm behind her legs and scooped her up in his arms, stooped to grab her crutch, and started toward her apartment.

"Put me down," she said, amazed at the power in his steady arms when the altitude made her breathless just walking to the kitchen.

"No problem." He hurried over the deck leading to her door. "You don't weigh much, do you? If you cook the way you ski, I can see why." He reached her door, set her down, watched as she fished her keys out of one of the pockets in her torn ski suit. When she found it he took it from her hand and opened the door.

A tiny roomful of packed boxes greeted them, and he stepped in behind her and looked around at the bare, impersonal walls, the matchbox kitchen, the open bedroom that could have passed as a closet. "I . . . I haven't had the chance to put everything away yet," she explained self-consciously. "There's not much space."

"This is where they make their employees live?" he blurted without thinking.

Marti snapped up her chin indignantly. "I happen

to like it. I could have had a bigger place, but I would have had to share it with three people. This suits me just fine."

Realizing that his astonishment had pierced her pride, Doug tempered the rest of his words. "Well, when everything's unpacked it could be cozy, I guess. But for tonight we'll stay at my place. It's a little more comfortable. Go change clothes."

"Doug, I can't."

"If you don't want me changing your clothes for you, go do it," he demanded, deciding it was high time he took control of this situation. "I'm tired of fighting you on this."

She wasn't certain if it was the altitude or the concussion that was making her dizzy, but suddenly she felt too weak to argue. All she wanted was to lie down, and at this point it made little difference where. Going into her room, she worked off her ruined ski suit, tossed it on the floor, and found a pair of jeans. After slipping on a soft pink sweater, she glanced in the mirror. Her hair was a mess and her face looked as if she'd been on a three-day drunk. She hobbled into her bathroom, brushed her teeth, raked out the tangles in her hair, and applied a touch of makeup just to avoid resembling death. *Why?* she asked herself when she was finished. The last thing she wanted was to be attractive to him, wasn't it?

Deciding her question was best left unanswered, Marti came out of her room. Doug's smile of approval told her exactly why she'd gone to the trouble.

"Much better," he drawled. Handing her the fake fur coat he had found in her closet, he helped her into it, opened the door, and picked her up again.

"Please," she said quickly. "I'd rather walk."

"It's too icy on the parking lot," he argued.

Becoming too weak to fight, Marti gave in and clasped her hands around his neck. It was distressing how secure his strong arms made her feel, and biting back her apprehension, she tried to hang her head back to keep it from throbbing.

"Put your head on my shoulder," he ordered. "It'll be more comfortable."

Reluctantly, she obeyed, closing her eyes. He smelled fresh, like the snowy outdoors, and the heat of his neck warmed her face. "I'll never be comfortable again," she whispered into his neck.

"Yes, you will," he assured her in a deep, calm rumble. "Very soon."

The soft sigh issuing from her lips sent a shiver down his back, and he glanced down at the flaxen hair flapping in the wind. She was so light, he thought. And it felt good holding her against him, feeling her curl into him as if he alone could provide comfort. Most women he knew demanded so much, but Marti Jackson seemed to want nothing. And, ironically, for the first time in months, he found himself wanting to give. He didn't blame her for having barriers, he thought. Women with looks like hers often had walls to protect them. Walls that often were more trouble to break down than the victory was worth. He doubted that was so in Marti's case.

He set her down when they reached his front door and led her in, turning on the lights and dropping his keys onto a table. She stood tentatively in the doorway between the foyer and the living room, fighting the sudden urge to turn and flee—pain or no pain—from

31

Doug's expensively furnished condo. No wonder he'd turned up his nose at her apartment. Cozy, he'd said. Wasn't that a term that polite rich people used for "sadly lacking"? She glanced back at him and assessed him for the signs she had missed. No diamond rings, no designer clothes, no high-priced dental work. Just a man. A man who owned a Colorado condominium worth twice more than the President's annual income. And that was clue enough that she had no business with him. Wasn't that the first clue she'd had that she didn't belong with Mike? Swallowing back the sense of déjà vu, she glanced around the luxurious condominium, decorated in earth colors. The white-cushioned sofa beckoned her in spite of herself, and finally she started toward it, taking in the gray bricks of the fireplace, the natural beams of the cathedral ceiling, the bare wood paneling, and the off-white carpet, all counterbalanced with brightly colored throw pillows and wall hangings and several well-groomed plants. A baby grand piano, covered with half-filled dirty glasses and ashtrays full of butts and ashes, sat in one corner facing the glass doors that looked out over the mountains. A guitar leaned against a wall next to a cluttered stack of sheet music. "Nice place," she said grudgingly as he went to the fireplace and turned on the gas, immediately producing soft, low flames. "It's about twelve times bigger than mine. Do you own it?"

"Yeah. It's comfortable." He took a log off the hearth and dropped it into the fire, then stood up, brushed off his hands, and started up the spiral staircase. "I think I'll go change. Sit down and get comfortable. The phone's next to the couch if you want to call your friend."

Dismissing thoughts of the tension and aggravation erupting between them, Marti sank onto the sofa, propped her foot next to her, and reached for the phone. She punched Amanda's number and left a message on her friend's machine that she was all right. If she knew Amanda, she was panicking over Marti's disappearance. Hanging up the phone, she leaned back. This, she decided, was the most comfortable she had been since she'd left Florida. No, she corrected herself. It was the most comfortable she'd been since she'd learned the truth about Mike. There had been no real rest, no real peace, since she discovered her fiancé with another woman and realized her engagement was a sham.

Marti closed her eyes and leaned her aching head back. She had never been one to run from her problems, and that was not what she was doing now. She was just always impatient for new beginnings, and she always cut endings as short as she could. What was the point in hanging around to listen to Mike's superficial pleas for forgiveness? Their relationship was over, and the sooner she put it behind her, the better. She sat up and let her eyes stray back to the staircase, wondering if Doug was meant as one of those beginnings or destined to be another quick ending. Time would tell, she thought, whether she wanted it to or not. It always did.

The sound of running water reached her ears, and she wondered if Doug had decided to shower. Glancing up, she saw him rounding the railing and descending the staircase. He looked transformed in his faded jeans and sneakers and his blue flannel shirt with the sleeves rolled up. She noted the dark mat of hair

33

where his shirt opened at the neck, and the well-developed muscles of his forearms as he slid his hands down the coiling banister. He seemed more human in his everyday clothes, more honest, and because of that Marti raised her defenses another notch. Men who seemed honest rarely were. "How you feeling?" he asked.

Marti smiled faintly. "Just shoot me and put me out of my misery."

"That bad, huh?" He came to the couch, stooped in front of her. "You like Jacuzzis?"

Was he kidding? Did he honestly think that a farmer's daughter would know whether or not she liked Jacuzzis? But then, he didn't know she was a farmer's daughter. "I can take them or leave them," she said finally. "Why?"

"Well, I have one upstairs. It'd do wonders for your aches and pains. You could prop your sprained ankle on the side to keep it dry, and then when you got out the rest of your muscles wouldn't feel quite so bad."

Marti's face reddened, warming beneath his emerald scrutiny. Did he really expect her to disrobe without a thought and take a bath with his help?

"I have a swimsuit here that I think would fit you," he said, as if reading her mind.

"A woman's swimsuit?"

Doug nodded. "A friend of mine left it here the last time she was in town."

The admission caused a tug of annoyance within her, and Marti fought it back, telling herself his love life was no concern of hers. Slowly her eyes stole to the staircase and she tested her judgment for an answer, but none came. Would she be taking advantage if she accepted his offer, or would he? And did it really matter in light of the pain throbbing through her injured body? She had never hurt in so many places at once, and Doug seemed harmless enough. For an instant she wondered if he would join her in the tub, wondered how he would look in swimming trunks, wondered if that skiing tan reached farther than his hands and face. Then, abruptly, she reprimanded herself and offered him a guarded smile. "Why not, if it'll really help ease the pain," she answered meekly, ignoring all the warnings that flooded through her.

Without a word Doug stood and scooped her up off the couch. She tried not to look at him as he carried her up the staircase, but it was difficult to avoid meeting his velvety green eyes. Trustworthy eyes, she thought. But then Mike's eyes had seemed that way too. She looked away, toward the bathroom coming into view, then glanced back at him again.

He slowed his pace to avoid stumbling from sheer distraction as he looked at her. The sight of those innocent eyes made him weak, and he searched for a comparison that would make her seem less intriguing. A blue-eyed doe was what she reminded him of, he thought, if there had ever been such a thing. The way she glanced at him under those heavy lashes, then quickly looked away, as if afraid of what she was seeing there. Amazing how that innocent way of looking at him stirred his most elemental emotions. For a moment he wondered if he should join her in the Jacuzzi, then thought better of it.

Hell, he thought, laughing inwardly. With any other woman he would never have suggested the swimsuit and would have stripped and joined her without a thought or any discussion. But Marti Jackson was not any other woman, and he would have to keep his desires in check to avoid frightening her away. For some reason that he could not pinpoint, he felt a stubborn determination to know her. It would take time, he thought, but good things were always worth waiting for. So were good women.

At the bathroom door he let her legs slide down his body almost in slow motion. Marti swallowed and dropped her eyes to his chest as his hand slid up her side to steady her.

"The swimsuit is next to the tub," he said in a raspy voice. "I'll go get you some aspirin while you change. And then I'll come help you get in without getting your ankle or wrist wet."

Nodding, she closed the door behind her. Leaning against it, she berated her heart for its adolescent fluttering, her hands for their obvious trembling, her resolve for its sudden crumbling. It was dangerous, it was frivolous, it was all the things she had believed she was strong enough to resist.

But Doug Duziak had caught her in a weak moment, and she swore to herself that she would keep that in mind, no matter what happened next.

CHAPTER THREE

Marti stood before the full-length mirror and stared in horror at the black slinky swimsuit she had just put on. She tugged on it to make sure her breasts were not fully exposed, for the neckline plunged in a V that didn't stop until it reached her stomach. The legs were cut almost to her waist, and the back was virtually nonexistent. *I can't let him see me in this,* she thought frantically. But, obviously, someone else already had. Chagrined, she wondered about the woman the suit belonged to. Were they occasional lovers or was there a commitment? Or were there several others just like her? Was she rich, like Doug?

Forcing her thoughts back to her own situation, Marti turned to the side and tried to see herself from a man's point of view. At least the parts of her so blatantly revealed were appealing, she mused.

Her eyes drifted to the Jacuzzi filled with hot, bubbling water that promised to take out some of the soreness. If only she had something else to wear. Even her underwear would be less revealing than this.

Doug knocked on the door. "You okay?" he asked.

"Yes," she called in a cracked voice. *Just play it cool, Marti,* she told herself. *People respond to you the way you respond to yourself. If you don't act self-conscious, then maybe he won't notice anything.*

Taking a deep breath, she limped toward the tub. "I guess you can come in."

The door opened and Doug took a step toward her, then stopped as he caught sight of her. All expression drained from his face, and he made a vain effort to swallow. "Here's the aspirin," he said after a moment, dropping two pills into her hand and giving her the glass of water. He cleared his throat as he watched her take them, surprised at the impact of desire that rushed through him at the sight of her. He had seen that she was beautiful already. But he had not been prepared for the perfection of her body—the long, shapely, tanned legs; the perfect curve of her hips; the small waist that he was sure could fit within the circle of his fingers; the sensuous swell of her breasts, covered just enough to stimulate the imagination, unbearably. He tried to refocus his thoughts as she set the glass down.

"Now," he said in a heavy raspy voice, "I think the thing to do here is to let me pick you up and lower you into the water. Be sure to prop your left leg and arm on these towels on the side of the tub so the swelling won't get worse, okay?"

Marti straightened and took a deep breath, hoping none of the swimsuit's cloth would shift when he moved her. "Okay," she said.

For another instant he stared at her, and she wondered if he was as uncertain of the security of the swimsuit as she. Without thinking, she raised her hand to her chest.

Doug cleared his throat. "You sure do more for that suit than its owner ever did," he whispered.

Marti took a deep, shaky breath and forced herself to meet his gaze. "She has interesting taste. Does this suit come with a whip and chains?"

He chuckled softly. "Probably, but she didn't bring them here." Sighing, he raked a hand through his hair. "Well, are you ready?"

Marti nodded and he came to her. She circled both arms around his neck as he lifted her. Their eyes came together for a flash of a second, and her heart bolted. She looked away and saw that the cloth covering her breasts *had* shifted. Quickly she reached for it and moved it back into place, and when their eyes met again—his pupils widening, though partially obscured by his heavy lids—she knew he had missed nothing.

Slowly he lowered her into the water until her right leg and arm steadied her. She kept her good leg bent and set her left one on the side of the tub to keep the heat from making her joints swell any more. "How's that?" he asked quietly as she settled back against the side.

Closing her eyes, she sighed as the hot bubbles coaxed the tension from her muscles. "Wonderful. It's just what I needed."

Doug smiled and stood up, drying his hands on a towel, his eyes trained on the arch of her body in the water.

As her body relaxed, Marti gave her mind free rein to lead her into thoughtless contentment. She hoped she could sustain this secure, peaceful feeling through the night, for nights were the worst. Funny how darkness sharpened pain.

Noting the shadow drifting over her features as the tension melted out of her expression, Doug sat on the ceramic tile next to the sunken tub and looked down at her. "Feeling better?"

"Much," she admitted. "I hope I'm not keeping you from your work or anything."

"No," he said, picking up her glass and rolling it against his palm. "I took the day off to do some skiing. I have other engineers who can take care of things."

"What kind of music do you record?" she asked.

"All kinds. Rock 'n' roll, country, gospel. A few jingles now and then."

She sank lower into the Jacuzzi, letting it cover her sore shoulders, comforting her no less than his voice did. "I couldn't help noticing the piano and guitar downstairs. Are you a musician too?"

"No, not really. I rewrite arrangements sometimes when I'm producing an album for someone who can't do that, and I do most of it at home."

"I've never met a recording engineer," she said. "I didn't know they were responsible for the arrangements."

"Just occasionally," he said. He smiled at the nervousness of their conversation and watched the long strands of her blond hair float around her on the surface of the bubbling water. Without thinking he dipped a finger in the water and lifted a wet strand. "Beautiful hair," he whispered, stroking it with his thumb. His eyes moved from the strand of hair to her eyes, brilliant and wide and surprised at the shift in conversation, then dropped to the wet swimsuit that lay like a second skin over her breasts. He fought the surge of desire shooting through him at the sight of the hard peaks of her nipples, telling him that beyond that transparent mask of indifference she felt a similar pull. Who was this woman, he thought with a swallow, who had practically dropped from the sky directly into his path? And where in his life would he put her, amid the complications, demands, and headaches? How did she fit into the parade of people that marched in and out of his life as if they owned it? *Somewhere,* he thought, for she was the first person in a long time that he had actually wanted to know.

Clearing his throat again, Doug tried to focus his thoughts on more practical matters. "You said you were starting your new job tomorrow. What do you do?"

"I'm going to be booking the entertainment for the two clubs here," she said. "That's what I did at the Unicorn's sister resort in Florida."

Surprise darkened his eyes. "Then we have related professions."

"In a way. Do any big names use your studio?"

"Several," he said. "The Clean Slate, Sushi Six, Trish Tanner—"

"Trish Tanner?" she cut in. "She's one of my favorites. I have most of her albums."

"She'd be flattered," he said. "You know, you're wearing her swimsuit."

"Oh." The word fell like lead between them, and she glanced down at the suit, thinking of the flamboyant bombshell that shared Doug's Jacuzzi when she was in town. A sick feeling swelled inside her. "Then you and Trish . . . ?"

"Are friends," he finished, somehow feeling as if it was dreadfully important to make that clear to her.

"We've known each other for a long time." Doug would have given anything to read Marti's thoughts as the silence grew between them.

Finally, when he could take no more of the tension, he got up off the floor. "You should probably get out now. It's not good to stay in for very long."

Marti started to move, but before she could slide up he had gathered her in his arms and was standing her up, sleek and wet before him, wrapping the towel around her shoulders. She took the edges from him and pulled them around her, aware that his eyes grazed the full mounds of her breasts, then dipped to her small hips and slim legs. She began to dry off self-consciously, carefully covering the breasts that gave her away. Her skin was red from the heat of the water, and the bruises were darker. She glanced up at him, and he backed toward the door.

An expressive smile broke the tension. "Well, I guess you can do the rest without me."

She nodded, suppressing her own answering smile, and he left her and closed the door behind him. This was crazy, she thought. The tension sizzling between them would have to be relieved somehow, and since she couldn't leave until morning it would probably get worse before it got better. She silently swore that she would not allow anything to come of it.

When he had carried her back down the stairs, she lay on the couch, relaxed after the soothing bath. Doug sat in a chair at right angles to the sofa, looking out the window at the magnificent beauty of the mountains, his eyes panning the view but seeing something else that she could not define.

"How long have you known Trish Tanner?" she

asked finally, in a voice carefully controlled to sound disinterested.

He began tapping his foot and folded his arms stiffly across his chest. "Ten, twelve years. I don't know."

Marti considered that for a moment, and tried to picture him with the glamorous singer. It was fitting, she thought. What man could resist her disarrayed beauty, her raspy voice, and the talent that enabled her to write such moving music and lyrics? The tune to her favorite song of all time played over in her mind. Marti had recently told a friend that "Fireworks and Roses," Trish Tanner's first hit song, had become her own theme song. The friend had tried to talk her out of believing the dismal, plaintive philosophy in the lyrics, but that friend hadn't known what it was to be alone. "The Rock 'n' Roll Prodigy of the Decade" Trish had been called after that song made number one on the *Billboard* Top "40." And she was a "friend" of Doug's. Something inside Marti wilted—the beginning of something she hadn't yet named—and left in its stead a cool feeling of defeat at a game she had never intended to play. "Do you think she'd consider doing a show here next time she's in town?" she asked in a hollow voice, hoping to mask her sudden melancholy.

Again Doug's face drained of feeling and he stood up and went to the window. "I doubt it. You could never pay her what she's used to, and she's not the most charitable person in the world. Besides, she comes to Breckenridge to hide out."

Something in his tone and his tight stance warned Marti to let the subject die, and sullenly she realized that she really did not want to know more. She watched his silhouette against the window and again wondered how often he had seen Trish in that skimpy swimsuit, and if he had bathed with her in the Jacuzzi. She wondered how close they must be for her to leave her clothes in his apartment and for such pensiveness to set in at the mention of her name. For the thousandth time she wished she had never met Doug Duziak, for already she could feel herself becoming attached.

He turned back to her and picked up his guitar. She closed her eyes as he began strumming it, but before she could name the familiar tune it had lulled her to sleep.

Marti didn't know how much time had passed when she woke to the sound of a piano. Opening her eyes, she saw Doug sitting before it with a cigarette in one side of his mouth, a pencil behind his ear, a few pages of staff paper propped on the stand that he stopped and wrote on every few bars, and several more pages wadded on the floor around him. His long fingers moved across the keys, creating a harmony that complemented the simple melody, making it a composition of raw emotion rather than creative intellect. He closed his eyes and dropped his head back as he played, and she sat up, awed at the feeling in his face, the sensuous way his body swayed to the tempo, the soft sound of his voice humming the melody. He paused for a moment, tapped out the beat with his finger, wrote the notes down. His fingers tinkered with the keys as he tried to remember a bar, and his green eyes sparkled with imagination when the notes came together. Each time his eyes closed, Marti wondered

44

what he saw. She wondered if he could see the muse that inspired him, and she longed—for a moment—to know this man, to have him share the beauty and depth of his world with her, to show her something more than the superficiality she'd known with Mike.

He stopped a moment, tapped his cigarette on the side of an ashtray, put it back between his lips, his eyes squinting through the smoke curling from his mouth. Glancing over his shoulder, he saw that she was awake. "Oh," he said, a glint of surprise in his eyes. He took the cigarette from his mouth and butted it in an ashtray. "I was just about to wake you."

"It was beautiful," she said, reluctant to disturb the almost reverent atmosphere. "Is it yours?"

He smiled and looked affectionately at the music. "Don't I wish. No, it belongs to one of my regulars. He's good with a melody and lyrics, but he can't manage the rest. So that's sort of where I come in when I'm producing one of his albums."

"I'm impressed," she said, admiration shining in her eyes. "You're very good. And your voice . . . why don't you record yourself?"

He shook his head and looked back at the ivory keys, stroking them with sensual fondness, though a memory suddenly shaded his eyes. "I'm no performer. I get my thrills making other people's songs sound good. I tried performing once, but I never could stand the idea of offering myself to a crowded roomful of people, for them to jeer at or have contempt for—"

"Or absolutely go wild over," Marti interjected quietly.

He stopped and gave her a soft smile. "Even that would make me miserably uncomfortable," he said.

"And there's not much point in recording if you don't like to perform. If I can't do something wholeheartedly, I'd rather not do it at all."

"But that was so beautiful . . ."

Her sincere expression made him laugh. He looked back down at the music and stacked the sheets carefully. "You really liked it, huh?"

"I really did. That piece made me feel . . . something."

As if she had uttered the password to some dimension she was unaware of, he turned back to her, his arrested expression driving the breath from her lungs. "Last week one of my engineers told me it was the most boring tune he'd ever heard."

"Before you had improved it and made it into a potential classic?" she asked.

He tilted his head, a slow smile spreading across his face with his sigh. "I think I'm falling in love," he laughed. "I've never known anyone with such exceptional insight."

Marti felt her cheeks growing warm and lowered her eyes. She attempted to laugh lightly.

Doug closed the piano and stood up.

"Don't stop because of me," she said quickly. "I didn't mean to interrupt your concentration."

"You didn't," he said, coming to sit beside her. "You've just made my day." Her eyes were still heavy with sleep, and her hair had dried in soft waves around her face, spilling over her shoulders. Again he lifted a strand and twirled it around his finger, his thumb caressing it. "I have to admit, that's the best work I've done in months. You seem to have inspired me."

"Me?" she asked. "What did I do?"

"I'm not sure," he said seriously, his eyes homing in on her lips as his voice lowered. "But I hope you'll let me return the favor someday."

"Come on," she hedged. "Look at all you've done for me today." Her hand strayed to her wrapped wrist. "I don't even think you know how much."

"All right," he conceded, his face moving closer to hers. "Then we're both indebted." His voice lowered to a whisper, and he watched her lips, his fingers climbing the strand of hair to her roots.

Marti swallowed, and her eyes widened when they locked with his. She felt as if he were offering her a taste of his magic world, and she was powerless to refuse. His fingers brushed under her hair, and his other hand rose to her face as his lips claimed hers.

Soft, she thought as her mouth opened beneath his. *His lips are so soft.* Her hand slid up his hard chest, and with her thumb she felt his pulse racing in his neck. Was she crazy, melting in the arms of another man so soon after her heartbreak? She raked her hands through his tousled hair, struggling to push the thought from her mind. His mustache brushed along the side of her mouth as he moved to make his kiss deeper, and his hands slid sensuously down to the sides of her breasts.

Marti sucked in a breath and pulled back, her hands trembling against his chest. "Doug," she breathed. He opened his eyes to hers, his lashes dark crescents hooding his eyes. "I . . . things are going too fast."

Too fast, he repeated mentally, wondering why the mild rejection didn't amuse him. Under any other circumstances and with any other woman, he would have

47

been well past the conquering stage by now. Yet here he was, willing to retreat for the sake of convincing her he was tame. Clearing his throat, he whispered, "Right. Too fast." His hand slid back up to her smooth face, and he studied her eyes, and a regretful grin broke across lips still wet with the taste of her. "Would you believe me if I told you I was just trying to take your pulse?" Were her eyes really that blue?

"I don't think that's the conventional way," she said. Was his mustache really that silky?

"No, it isn't the conventional way," he admitted softly. Reluctantly, he drew back slightly and said, "Anyway, your pupils look fine."

"And how is my pulse?"

He laughed easily, breaking the tension. "Yours is fine. It's mine I'm worried about."

Marti could have argued that hers was far from fine, but she was more interested in her effect on his.

"Well," he said, standing up. "You go on back to sleep and I'll wake you in a couple of hours."

She watched as he went back to the piano and began to play that same slow, drugging melody, and wondered how she was going to get her heart out of the mess it was leading her into this time.

CHAPTER FOUR

It was late night . . . or early morning. Marti was at home . . . or somewhere else. She was dreaming . . . or someone was trying to wake her. And she was tired. So tired . . .

"Wake up, Hot Dog."

The gravelly voice held its own fatigue, but the sound was comforting and curious, and Marti struggled to open her eyes.

Doug sat next to her on the couch, leaning over her, a hand on either side of her shoulders. His hair was sleep-disheveled, and his mustached smile was weary, and his eyes . . . She opened her eyes farther, savoring the insight that the first vulnerable moment of wakefulness can afford, and looked into those eyes. They were the color of jade in the dim light, and strangely they robbed the moment of its awkwardness. He was comfort and security. And she had nothing to fear from him.

A gentle hand brushed aside a wisp of hair, then adjusted the blanket that he had covered her with while she slept. "I had to wake you. Doctor's orders." The familiar cadence of Doug's voice cut into her sleepy soul and made her smile. "Come on. Open those pretty eyes. Let me see them."

Marti squinted up at him. "People who value their lives know better than to wake me in the middle of the night."

The warning left him undaunted. "Well, you know what they say up here. 'No guts, no glory.'"

She stretched her arms over her head and gave in to a yawn. "You were expecting glory for this?"

"I'd settle for undying gratitude," he admitted.

She smiled and dropped her hands to her stomach. "Can I get back to you on that?"

"Sure," he said. "I'll check again in two hours. Meanwhile, how do you feel?"

"Lousy. My head feels like a Mack truck is doing wheelies in it."

"I'll get you some more aspirin. Any other problems?"

"Yeah. My ankle hurts, my wrist throbs, I feel like I've—"

"Rolled down a mountain?"

"Exactly. I think I'm dying."

He whispered a laugh. "Marti, try not to be so brave."

Helpless to do otherwise, Marti laughed too. A spark seemed to catch between them, and suddenly the laughter died in a sighing expiration. And then they were serious, looking at each other as if they'd been intimate for years, and Marti felt more transparent than she'd been since the high school quarterback had told her that her crush on him was dreadfully obvious.

As if he saw something in her eyes that made him uneasy, Doug got up quickly. "I'll go get the aspirin."

He was gone in an instant, leaving Marti lying alone in the room lit only by a single lamp and a dying fire, wondering if she was so transparent that he recognized the chemistry stirring within her and didn't want to encourage it. She'd have to be more guarded, she told herself. But how could one be guarded sleeping in a stranger's condominium and being awakened by him every two hours? Sleep was a very intimate state, a very seductive state that replaced fortitude with vulnerability. And she hated being vulnerable.

"Here." His voice was soft when he came back with the aspirin and a glass of water. When she handed the glass back to him, he straightened the blanket again, the gesture so gentle and caring that she felt herself slipping under his spell. "Go back to sleep now," he whispered.

As if the order were couched in hypnosis, she curled obediently under the blanket and drifted back into a deep sleep.

From the groggy dimension between wakefulness and sleep, Doug felt his body tipping to the side, and abruptly he snapped himself upright. He'd always considered this easy chair comfortable, but tonight it was downright miserable. He leaned his head back and set his elbow on his thigh, propped over the chair's arm. It wasn't the first time he'd slept like this. But that was a long time ago, and this was different. Now he wasn't waiting in a backstage dressing room of a Las Vegas nightclub, waiting for his mother's set to finally end.

Tonight he was sitting in his own home, watching a gorgeous woman sleep on his couch.

He looked over at her, at the tangle of hair falling over her face, at the hands clasped under her chin like a child poised for prayer, at the bare foot with painted pink toenails peaking out from under the blanket. No one would ever believe his standoff behavior each time he had awakened her tonight. His resolve not to stir things up had weakened as the night wore on. At midnight he would have died to taste those moist lips again. At 2 A.M. he would have swum the English Channel to lie down beside her and feel her responding to his touch. But he had suffered through without making an advance. He hadn't even volunteered his bed to her for fear that she'd think he was making a lewd suggestion. Not that one hadn't crossed his mind. . . .

She turned over on the couch and her arm fell off the side. Another movement like that, he thought, and she'd wind up on the floor. And that wouldn't do her injuries any good.

He dropped his feet to the floor and set his elbows on his knees. Wearily he rubbed at the fatigue in his eyes and watched her readjust her head. She was miserable, even in her sleep, and she would feel worse in the morning. She needed to sleep in a bed.

He stood up and felt the sudden wave of exhaustion pulling at his body. He didn't remember ever being so tired. Only a crazy man would volunteer to do this after an all-night studio session and a day on the slopes, he told himself. But he'd suspected himself to be losing his faculties several times that day. He went to the couch and gazed down at her. Her golden hair spanned out over the cushion, and her lashes crescented peacefully against her cheek. No, he wasn't crazy, he told himself. Not crazy at all. Just a little enchanted.

Slipping his arms under her shoulders and knees, he lifted her, blanket and all, and coaxed her face to rest against his shoulder. The warmth she exuded had been foreign to him for years, and he rebuked his body for responding to it. *You don't need this, Duziak,* he told himself. *You have enough problems without this.*

But warnings had never had much impact on him, even when they came from a side of himself that usually proved to be right. Lowering his cheek to her hair, he started up the stairs.

When he reached the bed in the center of a large, masculine bedroom, he stooped and pulled back the covers, then laid her down. She breathed a soft sigh as she curled up on the bed, and he pulled away the blanket and covered her with the bedclothes.

A strange emotion washed over him as he stood back to look at her. It wasn't desire, really. At least that wasn't all it was. It was more of a protective feeling that wasn't likely to go away with the morning light. And he wasn't sure he wanted it to.

Without thinking or censoring his intention, he leaned over and pressed a kiss on her temple. And suddenly every siren in his body rang out in warning —warning that this emotion did not come without a very high price, and that paying it might already be beyond his choices.

A ringing sound invaded Marti's sleep, pulling her out of her cocoon of comfort and forcing her to open her eyes. She was in Doug's bed, tucked carefully under the covers, and the alarm clock was screaming for attention. She sat up in bed, trying to adjust her eyes, and brought a warm hand to her aching head. The clock continued to blare urgently, and she looked around and saw that it lay on the bed next to her.

Between her and Doug.

She caught her breath and her hand froze on the clock's chrome rim. When its ringing increased in volume she turned it off and stared at Doug the way one would stare at an alien that suddenly appeared out of nowhere. He was sound asleep on the top of the bedcovers, sprawled out, and still wearing his shoes. He had obviously brought her to bed, tucked her in, and then collapsed, himself. Marti couldn't help smiling at the innocence with which he'd fallen asleep beside her.

Pulling out of bed quietly to keep from waking him, she hopped to the bathroom and checked her eyes. When she was satisfied that she was fine she made her way back to the bed and reset the clock. Then she took the loose blanket he had used to cover her downstairs, the blanket now wadded on the floor, and draped it over him.

She got back into the bed and lay facing him for a while. He was a gentle man, and yet this morning she had been certain there was no such thing. She couldn't remember ever having someone take such pains to see that she was comfortable. He had given until he was exhausted, with no real expectations of getting anything in return.

Marti reached out and stroked his hair out of his face. Maybe he would get something in return, after all, she thought vaguely as sleep drew her under again. Maybe the whole day had been predestined. And maybe his wealth wasn't symbolic of disloyalty, dishonesty, and restlessness. Maybe he would be different. . . .

A difference in the shadows hovering in the room told Marti it was morning, and she saw the earliest rays of the sun beaming through the window when she opened her eyes. Doug lay next to her watching her wake.

"Hi," he whispered.

"Hi," she said.

"Looks like I didn't do my job very well," he said in a sleepy, gravelly voice. "Slept right through the last alarm."

"I heard it," she said.

They smiled at each other for an awkward moment, like lovers who weren't sure what to say the morning after. Did they move closer or farther apart? Did they speak with familiarity or with the coolness of strangers? Did they refer to the closeness they'd shared or ignore it in hopes it would disappear in the sunshine?

Unaccustomed to such awkwardness in an unprecedented situation, Marti quickly sat up and brushed her hair back with splayed fingers. As if to follow her without seeming to, Doug propped himself on an elbow and gave her an apologetic look, wondering if her abrupt movement meant he had offended her.

"I didn't mean to fall asleep up here," he said. "I just—"

"It's okay." She turned back to him and tried to relax. "It's your bed, after all."

"Still, I . . ."

His voice faded as their eyes locked again, and finally he sat up. His hair looked as if he'd just come in from a windstorm, and his eyes, unguarded and freshly awake, were the color of warmth.

"You know, it isn't like anything happened."

"I know," she said. "It's okay." She stood up and straightened her clothes, as if she wore a freshly pressed dress rather than a crumpled sweater and wrinkled jeans. Her eyes strayed to the clock. "Look at the time," she said. "I have to go home. I start my new job today."

"Are you sure you feel up to it? You could stay a little longer . . ."

She stemmed his invitation with an outstretched hand. "No, I really have to go. I feel fine. Really."

Feeling helpless to keep her there, Doug watched her hop on one foot to the bathroom. Somehow he knew she wouldn't want him to help her—to touch her—this morning.

When she came out he saw that she had brushed her hair and washed her face, and her clothes still hung on her body, hiding the gracious curves and soft flesh that he had dreamed about last night.

He followed her, hands in his pockets, as she hobbled down the stairs. When she went to the chair that held her things, he reached down to help her.

"You want me to . . . ?"

"I can get . . ."

The words came out simultaneously, and Doug's hands plunged back in his pockets.

"You've gone way beyond the call of duty," Marti

said, unable to meet his eyes as her cheeks colored with a rosy glow. "I really appreciate it."

He looked around him, as if grasping for some way to make her stay. Wasn't she leaving something important, something that would at least bring her back later? When she began to pull on her coat he steadied her crutch and helped her. "You won't even stay for breakfast? Nothing?"

She smiled at the forlorn, abandoned look on his face, almost as if he were the one with the injuries and had grown dependent on her help instead of the other way around. "I'm not hungry, no. I really have to get home and get ready. I have to be at work in an hour."

He gave her a dejected smile. "Well . . . good luck. I hope it goes well."

"Thanks." She stood looking at him for a moment, battling the urge to reach up and press a kiss on his morning-stubbled jaw, to slide a finger across the silky mustache defining his lips. But instead she wrenched her eyes away from the expectancy in his and started for the door.

"Can I . . . will you let me walk you home?"

"I'm fine"—she turned back to him before opening the door—"and I have to get used to this sooner or later."

He raked his hand through his hair and took the doorknob, letting an instant icy wind swirl around them as he opened it. "I . . . I guess."

She started out, bracing herself against the cold wind slapping her face and scratching her lungs and the feeling of emptiness suddenly encompassing her. "Well . . . bye. And thanks again."

"Don't mention it," he said, leaning idly against the

jamb. "If I ever get a concussion, I'm sure you'll do the same for me."

"Yeah." She tried to laugh but failed, and finally started down the stairs, wishing that he'd go back inside and close the door and make this easier for her. He was someone she'd met yesterday. Someone who'd rescued her and taken care of her. That was all. No different than a doctor. He was *still* a stranger. Not a lover she was having trouble saying good-bye to. Not someone she was falling in love with.

She heard the sound of the door closing and stopped. Slowly she turned around, just to see, she told herself. Just to see . . .

And she saw. Doug was standing at his window, watching her. Their eyes met, embraced, fell apart. And finally Marti forced herself to turn and walk away.

Doug sat in his studio a week later and cursed himself for thinking about her again. He had promised himself that he would wait for her to make the next move. Didn't passiveness always work on women? Didn't that attitude of you-know-how-to-find-me always make them determined to come after him? Apparently Marti didn't know the rules of his game, he thought miserably, issuing a deep, despairing laugh. Wasn't this aggravating feeling inside him nothing more than an illusion created by a lonely heart and a jaded soul? He ran tired hands down his face and tried to wipe the image of Marti limping away from him out of his mind so that he could concentrate on the man crooning pitifully into the microphone. Distraction wasn't going to get him anywhere in a session like this.

He swiveled away from the window separating the raised control room from the vocal booth at Duziak Productions. Looking over his shoulder at Reed, the young man who assisted the studio engineers in technical chores, he frowned. "I'm good at what I do," he said in a bland voice, "but I'm not sure I can make this guy's voice sound passable."

Reed kept his features cool for the sake of the man who watched them while he sang. "You'll have to work magic, all right," he agreed. "But the rest of the tracks are pretty tight."

"That's only because we talked him into using our studio musicians," Doug said, turning back toward the vocal booth behind the soundproof glass while he made some adjustments on the console. The song would be salvageable in spite of the poor vocals, he thought. Already he had run double tracks on the voice to "fatten" the sound, and adding a touch of reverb and a slight delay might distract from the voice itself. But there was no foolproof method of making a bad singer sound like a good one. Not even with twenty-four tracks and a fortune's worth of equipment.

Reed set his foot on a chair and leaned over to tie one of his stained suede boots. "Well, at least this is the last take."

"At least," Doug said with a decided look of enthusiasm. Then he could think about the next step he would take with Marti. As much uncertainty as he felt, he did at least know that there'd be another step. Even if *he* had to take it.

When the "singer" was satisfied with his final effort, Doug played back the raw tape that he would later mix into a harmonious—and hopefully less irritating —blend of sounds. But his mind wasn't on it today.

He thought of gossamer threads of silken hair as he automatically adjusted the sounds on each track, adding volume to the piano, lowering the bass drum. He thought of crystal eyes as he brought up the over-dubbed guitar lead and absently tested different ways of improving the vocals.

Moments later, his foremost desire was to rid the studio of the musicians, who would linger there indefinitely if he let them. He wanted to think. He wanted to sort out truth from fantasy. He wanted to decide how he'd make Marti fall in love with him. So, in the way of the high school coach clearing a smoke-filled bathroom of its daily assembly, he ushered his friends out the door with a half-baked explanation about having to care for a sick friend.

"Is that sick friend by any chance Trish?" Reed asked at the door.

"No, why?"

Reed gave an insouciant shrug and pulled on his leather gloves. "Well, I heard her tour ended a couple of days ago. I figured she'd be real sick after her last album was such a bomb."

Doug grimaced at the reminder and pulled out a cigarette. "It wasn't so bad." He paused to light it, then blew out a soft cloud of smoke. "And if you do see her, I'd appreciate it if you wouldn't mention it to her. She's not in the best of moods lately."

"Then you've heard from her?"

In his usual evasive manner, Doug sidestepped the question. "We keep in touch."

Reed cocked his brow perceptively—at least *he*

thought it was perceptive—and left the studio. Doug pulled the heavy door shut and went back to the control room. He didn't want to think about Trish. He wanted to think about Marti.

Why couldn't he get her off of his mind? he asked himself, taking the cigarette from his mouth and blowing a long breeze of smoke while he tapped his thin lighter on his knee. His thumb grazed his lip, and he hunched over the console, staring at the knobs and buttons and seeing Marti's face when she'd thanked-him-very-much a week ago and left, as if it was a final ending to their brief acquaintance.

Why wasn't that enough to stop him from wanting to go after her? Because she intrigued him, he told himself. Because she haunted him. Because she moved him.

He thought of the intensity and uncensored emotion on her face when he'd found her awake on his couch early that night, and the way she had praised his work and made him believe it. And he thought of how he'd felt the next morning when he'd awakened and found that she had covered him up in his sleep, as if her first thought upon finding him sleeping next to her was not anger or indignation, as he would have imagined, but concern that he was cold.

Putting out his cigarette, Doug stood up and grabbed his coat. Suddenly he knew what it was that was driving him crazy. He had left it all unfinished. He had rescued her, had nursed her through the night, and then sent her out into the cold all alone. That was it. He felt responsible, and he had to check on her to make sure that she wasn't feeling bad or that she didn't need anything or that he couldn't help her get somewhere. It was his duty. . . . It was his right.

And he was not going to let her take that away from him with a simple thank-you and a farewell smile.

Marti sighed with relief when her workday came to an end, and she could at last leave behind her gruff boss, Jack Crebbs, who bore a striking resemblance to the cover boy of *Mad* magazine and had the personality and good nature of Attila the Hun. Zipping her coat, she limped out into the main corridor of the Unicorn lodge and stopped to pull out her gloves.

"Hi, Hot Dog."

Her head snapped up at the welcome voice, and she saw Doug leaned back against the wall, one booted leg hiked up. In spite of herself, she smiled like a teenager who'd just been granted a wish. "Where did you come from?" she asked.

One side of his mustache tipped upward in a self-conscious grin. "Oh, nowhere. I was just walking by and thought I'd stand here and rest awhile."

Marti's eyes sparkled and she nodded dubiously. "Oh, you did, did you? Do you always stroll by the office end of the lodge?"

His shoulders rose innocently and his grin became broader. "Every chance I get."

She pursed her lips to suppress her knowing smile. He looked more handsome than she'd been remembering at decidedly inconvenient times during the day. His hair had a fresh-washed sheen that made her want to run her fingers through it, and his eyes glistened like emeralds against his tanned face. His body radiated warmth rather than outdoor cold, testifying to the fact that he'd been "resting" beside her office for quite some time.

"So how've you been?" he asked finally.

"Better."

He tried not to smile quite so foolishly. "So how's your job?"

"I'll get used to it," she said.

"Booked any good bands?"

"A few. The work's exciting. The atmosphere is a little chilly, though. My boss mumbles all day about it being a terrible image for a ski resort to have a woman on crutches working in the offices. He makes me hide my crutch in a closet and doesn't let me stand up all day."

"I *knew* you needed me," Doug proclaimed triumphantly. "I was in my studio and I had this sudden clairvoyant feeling that you were in need of another rescue. So I rushed right over."

Her brow arched with amusement. "I thought you said you were taking a walk," she reminded him.

He stepped toward her and lifted a lock of her hair, watched the tendril curl around his finger as his teeth clamped over his smile. "I did. Musta walked a mile waiting for you to come out."

She watched her hair play like a soft sunbeam over his rough finger. "Why didn't you just come in?"

He dropped his hand on her shoulder, slid it down her arm. "Same reason I let a week pass without talking to you," he admitted wryly. "I didn't want to seem too obvious."

An alarm in her mind warned her to pull away from his touch, but she chose not to heed it.

"So, you want to go eat? I could show you the town, we could listen to the music, visit the tourist traps."

"You really don't have to . . ."

He took her hand and lowered his teasing face to hers. "Marti, don't make me beg."

She swallowed. "Well, since you put it that way . . ."

He slipped his arm around her shoulders and drew her against him as he led her out of the lodge. "You won't regret it," he promised.

And she didn't. In fact, it was the most fun she'd ever had. It didn't matter that the temperature was four degrees or that the snow fell in continuous flurries as they made their way down Main Street and in and out of shops. She swallowed her inhibitions when he led her into the small Lincoln Mall and into the Bahnhof Shop, where they sang for a free pair of goggles. They stumbled, giggling, over the chorus to "I Want to Hold Your Hand," complete with invisible microphone and badly mixed harmony, then caught a Breckenridge shuttle to the slopes, where Doug insisted on taking her on a sleigh ride. But when one of the horses came down with a bout of "upset stomach" after only a few steps, and the tipsy driver refunded their money, Marti found herself collapsing against Doug in a fit of cold shivers and hysterical laughter. Then he took her to Beaver Run at the base of Peak Nine, where the Copper Top was crowded with thawing skiers relaxing with hot-buttered rums and other spirits, to the Jim Croce-style music of the happy-hour entertainment. And then they ate pasta to their heart's content at St. Bernard's Inn, and talked about insignificant things that seemed extremely significant, and learned that they had the same irrational passion for cheese cake, cinnamon tea, the Beatles, and Katharine Hepburn movies. Thus having established what their instincts told them was the flawless groundwork for a relationship, Doug took them back to his condo for tea.

He laughed to himself as he watched her beside him on the shuttle. She didn't need anyone to look after her, he could see now. So why had he spent the entire week thinking of the way that black swimsuit had clung to her breasts or the way her nipples had hardened when he'd touched her? And how had he convinced himself this morning that the reason he couldn't concentrate on his session was that he was worried about her? *Face it, Duziak,* he told himself. *It's not her bruises you're interested in.*

He watched her scratching at the frost on the inside of the window, inhibiting her view outside. God, she was gorgeous. Her honey-colored hair fell across one side of her face, and she absently pushed it behind an ear. Her blue eyes seemed even larger than they had the first time he'd seen her on the slopes. Now they seemed less self-conscious, more defined, like ocean waves on a sunny day when the sky was clear. Her cheeks were a healthy pink, but her skin was so fair that she almost looked fragile. He doubted that she was. *Damn,* he thought, making himself look away. *She's just a woman.* So why was his heart pounding mercilessly, and why did he want to reach over and turn her around to him and kiss her until her heart raced too?

You're in trouble, Duziak, he told himself with a smile as she looked over at him like a longtime lover, making his heart plummet. *Bigger trouble than you've ever known.* But he'd always liked living dangerously.

CHAPTER FIVE

Marti welcomed the comfortable elegance of Doug's condominium when they finally made their way back there. Somehow, in light of the simplicity and down-to-earth manner Doug had in approaching things, his life-style didn't seem quite as intimidating as first it had. Marti and Doug spent the evening becoming friends, but a lingering tension hung in the air, promising that beyond friendship there might be no turning back, and that they were already crossing that dangerous threshold. She had told herself she was better off not hearing from him all week, and had convinced herself that the explosive chemistry between them had been only in her imagination. Now she knew that the only thing she had imagined was her strength in avoiding that attraction.

When Doug went to the kitchen to put on the water for tea, Marti wandered to his piano and looked at the music on it, covered with penciled-in notes in his peculiar slanted scrawl with curling tails and elaborate notations. It had been years since she'd taken piano lessons, but curiosity compelled her to sit down and try the music with her good hand. She picked it out slowly, stopping and starting over, trying to make sense of the composition before her.

Before she knew he was in the room, Doug was leaning over her, playing the troublesome notes on the bass clef as she played the melody with her right hand.

His face was inches from hers, and she could smell the clean scent of his after-shave and the faint mint and tobacco smell of his breath. She smiled up at him as the song came together, but her shaky fingers continued to hit the wrong notes.

Self-consciously, she pulled her fingers from the keys and touched her chest. "I'm sorry," she said. "It's been a long time."

He took her place with his right hand, enclosing her in his arms. "I'll play it," he said, his voice unnervingly close to her ear. His chest brushed her back when he leaned toward the piano, toward her. His long fingers moved with ease and control as he played the poignant, romantic piece. When his hands moved closer together Marti was inexorably caught in his embrace, caught like a lonely animal who has found a home, caught like a wary beast who should have known better. The movement of his fingers was hypnotizing, the melody magical. He swayed lightly to the tempo, moving her with him, and she felt his face brushing against her hair. Her heart fluttered and she wanted to turn and look into his eyes and see the melody as much as she felt it.

With lowered lids, she turned her head. The movement brought her closer to Doug as her cheek brushed his, meeting the texture of stubble on his chin. His eyes followed her face until she looked into them, and his fingers slowed to a stop as his lips lowered to hers.

In Marti's mind the music continued to play. It followed him, she thought, and each time he kissed her he offered it to her. Her mouth opened, and his tongue moved slowly against hers. She felt as if her bones had turned to liquid as his hand moved from the keyboard to her neck and through her hair. She touched his face, memorizing the high cheekbones and the slope of his brow, tracing the line of his jaw and the soft spot of his neck where his pulse hammered a message of desire.

Doug heard a new melody as Marti responded to his kiss—a melody that had always been in the back of his mind. He heard it loudly now: it was as lovely as she. He framed her face with his hands and moved her head, deepening his kiss. How would it feel, he wondered, to undress her and hold her against him? The lovemaking, the exhilaration, the aftermath . . . His hand lowered to her breast.

Marti caught it and pulled back. Controlling her breath, she shook her head. "Stop. No."

Doug moved his hand but continued to hold her with a firmness that said it was not going to be easy to brush him off. "I'm sorry. I moved too fast."

"Yes, you did," she said quickly, with an echo of disappointment lacing her voice. Why? Why had he ruined it? She was falling for him, and she had known him only two days. This was only their second kiss, and it melted her so absolutely that she felt herself slipping away again, leaving her wounds open and aching. Wounds that needed more healing time before scarring completely. But it was her fault she was so vulnerable to him. Doug had only reacted to what he

69

knew was there—the feelings he had aroused. So why did she feel so frightened?

His arms folded gently around her, and he pressed his forehead against hers. "I'm sorry. I really am. It's just that you're so . . . so different." The last words faded to a whisper as his lips claimed hers again.

Marti started to back away, but her limbs were immobile. She couldn't help reacting to him, and it was as obvious as sunshine in an opaque blue sky that he was aware of it. Just as the kiss deepened, he pulled reluctantly away, ending it with one moist brush of his lips.

Again, his forehead rested against hers. "I'm not an animal," he whispered. "I'll wait until you're ready."

Marti dropped her eyes to his lips. "It might be a long wait."

"I'm a patient man," he said softly. Then his lips descended on hers again, and time stood still as his kiss set its own tempo in her mind.

The fact that they had discussed going no further and made a definite decision gave Marti an odd feeling of security, though his hands stole down her back, pulling her tighter against him as his kiss grew more meaningful, more urgent, more virile. She told herself she was in control, despite the quivering in her legs and the painful pounding of her heart in rapid sync with his. She could stop it when she chose, she assured herself. Until bare skin met bare skin, she would be safe.

Bare skin against bare skin. The image started a yearning ache in her core, a fire in the pit of her stomach. His hands pressed harder against her, massaging and kneading while the soft, wet, demanding pressure of his mouth pushed her back until her throat arched. It seemed that he knew she was putty in his arms as long as he held her mouth captive and continued with the Dionysian dance that intoxicated her.

The feeling was new to Marti. She had known love and even passion, but the mindless abandonment of rationality was a first. Timidly, she ran her hands up his broad ribs, testing, knowing, and with each touch he moved in a way that sent sparks flying through her. Her hands rose between them, slowly climbing to circle his neck, and her breath came in gasps.

The sound of his breath sent shivers down her neck, and pulling back, he opened his eyes, the reality and brilliance of them doing nothing to dispel the passion. But somehow, she knew it was over.

His warm eyes did not probe for more. She saw no test of wills, no conniving of passion. He had no intention of going on, despite the fact that they both knew her resolve had crumbled.

Stroking the blond hair spanned around her shoulders, he smiled at the unmasked disappointment in her eyes. "I just wanted to give you something to think about until you're ready," he whispered.

"You're good at this, aren't you?"she asked, dazed.

"I know what I'm doing," he conceded.

"Lots of practice, huh?"

"Enough."

The admission left a sour note in the wake of tenderness and teasing. Just how much of this was a game? she wondered. "And how do the ladies usually react in this situation?" Her tone still held a playful note, camouflaging the irritation she felt.

He grinned and played along. "They attack me and beg for more."

"Do they?" Her words held less amusement.

"Yes. They start dragging my clothes off and throwing themselves at me—"

"Is that what you expect me to do?"

He shrugged as if giving in. "If you must, you must," he teased.

The color creeping up her neck corresponded to the brittle sound of her voice, cluing him that they had gone beyond teasing.

His cocky expression disappeared. "Hey, I was just kidding."

"Were you?"

He looked alarmed. "Marti, we were joking. Both of us. You started it with that question about the ladies. How was I supposed to answer that?"

She swallowed and looked down at her hands. "Are there a lot of them?"

He laughed, astounded. "No, of course not. I'm not the type to roll from one bed to another. Marti, I like you. Why are you so set on believing I'm some kind of playboy?"

For a moment she wrestled with the question, searching for an honest answer. "Because of Trish Tanner," she answered finally.

Doug withdrew his hand and stood up. "What about Trish?"

"She leaves her bathing suit here and uses your Jacuzzi."

"You used my Jacuzzi, too, but I haven't slept with *you*, have I?" He heaved a deep breath and stepped toward her. "Look, we don't have to talk about Trish. She has nothing to do with this."

"Yes, she does. We were talking about the other women in your life."

He set his hands on his hips and looked at her, a perplexed expression on his face. "And why is that? To divert my attention from you?"

Marti sighed. "I just want to know if you're involved with her. That's all."

He swiveled and went to his glass doors and peered out on to the balcony. "This is ridiculous."

"Are you involved with her or not? It's a simple question."

When he turned back to her his eyes seemed cold. Something in his taut face told her to let the subject die, that the price wasn't worth the answer. But still she pressed on. "Answer me."

"Involved how?"

"Involved!" she repeated, knowing instinctively what his hedging meant.

"We're friends," he said in a cool voice that made her feel it was none of her business. He went to the piano, and closed the fall board loudly. His face was hard when he turned back to her. "I've known Trish for years."

The tone of his voice supplemented his words, and suddenly Marti felt she knew where she stood with Doug. It *was* a game to him, and she was the pawn. The pretty little Southern virgin that provided a distracting challenge to a man bored with the toys that wealth could buy. He was no different than Mike or any other man she'd ever known, except that he'd been a bit bolder in his assault of her heart.

73

Without another word she stood up and limped to the piano, where her crutch leaned, then went to the rack beside the door and got her coat.

"Are you leaving?" Doug demanded.

"Yes," she said, slipping into her coat. "I have things to do."

"But it's not late."

"I've had a long day," she returned.

"You don't have to go now." His voice was suddenly softer, and he grabbed the edge of the door when she opened it. "At least let me walk you home."

"I do have to go now," she said, "and I'll make it just fine. Good-bye."

A gust of icy wind slapped her hair against his face, and he stood in the doorway watching her make her slow, careful descent on the steps, then trudge over the ice across the parking lot. *Duziak, you're a damned fool,* he told himself, slamming the door with the force of self-reproach. There must have been a better way of handling the question about Trish. If he'd been prepared for it, he could have convinced her that there was nothing like she suspected between them. But the question had caught him off-guard, and he knew that his evasiveness had been written all over his face.

"Damn it!" he shouted, banging his fist against his foyer wall. When would his relationship with Trish stop haunting him, intruding on every area of his life? When would he ever have the courage to end it?

The whistling of the kettle attacked his senses, and storming into the kitchen, he yanked the kettle off the stove and threw it into the sink. What had Marti been thinking when she'd left? Probably that he was some kind of cad who got his kicks arousing, then discarding, women. When all along he had held back only to avoid frightening her away. Yet he had done that anyway.

He went back to the piano, threw open the fall board, and stared at the keys, as if they threatened him, for that was where he'd kissed her, when she'd been sitting on the bench between his arms. Dropping his elbows heavily on the keyboard and striking a violent, furious chord, he lowered his forehead to his palms. She was different. She was innocent. She was beautiful. And before he'd even had the chance to know her, he had probably lost her.

That thought still sat heavy in his heart when Doug, watching from the balcony off the side of his apartment, saw Marti limp out of her condo and down to the parking lot where the shuttle bus stopped. Holding the crutch pad with both hands, Marti kept her weight on one foot and gazed up the drive. Her hair was French braided down her back, and a furry pair of earmuffs hugged her ears.

A family with two preschoolers clad in snowsuits as wide as they were tall passed on the way to their car, and Doug watched the amused smile on Marti's face when the smaller child pointed at her injury and stopped to ask a question Doug could not hear. Nodding, Marti leaned over and pulled up her pants leg, showing him the bandage around her ankle, at which the child called his brother to come look. When the two children waddled off after their parents, Doug watched Marti prop her elbow on her crutch and rest her chin on her palm, a wistful look passing over her eyes as she stared after them. The need on her face tugged at his heart, matching some need of his own which he could not name. As he studied her a new feeling of resolve overcame him. She was not like the other women he knew. How she was different escaped him. But, somehow, he vowed to find out. Despite what she might think, they were not finished yet.

Just as the shuttle bus approached the stop Doug went back in for his coat and hurried out the door. Running surefootedly across the parking lot, he reached the door of the bus and hopped on.

Marti coiled tighter into herself when she saw Doug's tall figure climbing into the bus. With a quick pan of the passengers, he found her, his eyes apologetic and unsure as he started toward her, but she only turned away to gaze out the window. When he slipped into the seat beside her he didn't say a word.

After being shifted into gear, the bus started to circle the lot and drive back up the hill toward the lodge, and finally Doug gave her a sidelong glance. "Where're you heading, Hot Dog?" His voice was soft, teasing, casual compared to the heat just before they had parted yesterday.

Marti kept her eyes trained on the scenery outside her window. "The slopes. I just got off work and I'm not used to being cooped up, so I thought I'd go watch the skiers."

"I could have driven you. I have my Porsche here, you know."

"It isn't your responsibility to see that I'm entertained or to chauffeur me in your Porsche," she mumbled, looking out the window as the bus came to a halt in front of the lodge and the waiting shuttle to the slopes.

76

Doug wondered if it was bitterness he heard in her utterance of the word *Porsche,* but he shook off the thought. Why would his Porsche make her angry? When she stood up and got her crutch Doug was forced to move out of her way. He followed her off the bus, racking his brain for a way to break through the new wall she'd constructed since she'd left last night. When they were on concrete again he took her aside, away from strangers' ears, and lowered his voice to just above a whisper. "I don't consider it responsibility. I like being with you. Let's ride back to the condos and I'll drive you to the slopes."

Marti avoided his direct, disarming gaze and tried to remind herself why it was foolish to cultivate the chemistry between them. "Look, Doug, you're a nice man. You've been very helpful to me since I've been here, but I don't need any more help."

He touched her waist with a warm, coaxing hand and tipped his face down to hers.

"I'm not trying to help you," he rumbled. "My motives are absolutely selfish."

"That's just it," she answered with great effort. "I'm not interested in a relationship right now. I need to be alone."

"Nobody needs to be alone," he said. The steam of his breath mingled with hers in the freezing air.

Marti took a step back, forcing him to drop his hand to his side. "You don't understand. You don't even know me. I'm not what you think I am. A week ago I was engaged, and today I'm standing in Breckenridge, Colorado, with a new job, a new life . . ." Her voice fell off, and she took a sustaining breath and looked into the distance. "It has nothing to do with you. Really."

Doug's perusal grew more probing, and the disappointment etching the lines of his face stirred regret that she had no time to understand.

"The shuttle is about to leave," she said dolefully. "I'd better get on."

"When will I see you again?" His question came with apprehension as he watched her amble toward the line forming at the door of the bus.

"I don't know," she said wearily. "There's really no point, Doug. Just let it go, okay?"

His stance did not waiver, and she turned from those soft eyes that threatened to break through her defenses, and climbed onto the bus. When she found a seat she glanced out the window for one last look, but he had already gone.

A strange feeling of loss, different than the one she'd felt with Mike, took hold of her as the bus huffed up the mountain, and hope, once again, slipped like Florida sand through her fingers. She must be a masochist, she told herself. Otherwise, why had she set herself up for another fall with a man she hardly knew?

It was the empty feeling where a flurry of activity over her wedding was supposed to be, she decided. It was the loneliness after months of companionship with someone she thought she could trust that was getting to her. It was the chill of deception, the ache of betrayal. But it was not Doug.

The bus roared to a halt beside the Beaver Run resort. Marti stood up and waited for the laughing, vacationing groups of friends and couples in heavy ski attire to file off of the bus before she made her way out.

The icy assault of wind almost made her turn back, but as she had forced herself to make the move to Colorado despite her misgivings, she forced herself to limp toward the outside deck of the Copper Top, where the slopes were in full view. She dusted the snow off of a chair and sat down, looking up at the exhilarated skiers whisking down the Lower Lehman run. The joy and adventure were supposed to be as great for her. But she should have known that making plans was a certain way to have them come crashing down around her.

And she should know that sparkle and soft words from a wealthy man with secrets meant only one thing. It meant that pain was on the way.

Doug sat in the dark, empty bar and stared down at the drink before him. The ice cubes were melting, but he didn't seem to have a taste for the liquor in the glass. Instead, he let the music set his mood as two voices on the bar's turntable crooned about losin' that lovin' feeling. It was ridiculous, he thought, sitting here brooding over a woman he'd only known for a few days. But they weren't strangers, a voice inside insisted. He had watched her sleep, he had watched her hurt, he had watched her being brave. He had awakened next to her, had touched her hair, had warmed to her smile.

Planning a wedding one minute, then starting over the next, she'd said. It wasn't anything personal. He breathed a dry laugh and thought how ironic the whole thing was. He had wanted to stay unattached. He had not wanted to be interested in anyone. And the next thing he knew he had found himself an accident-prone beauty with a broken heart and a sign across her forehead that said "No trespassing." Which, of course, made him all the more determined to do just that.

"What are you doing here?" The husky, weary woman's voice drew him out of his reverie, and Doug looked up into a pair of dark glasses. Trish Tanner's dark glasses.

"Trish . . ." He stood up and regarded the disheveled elegance in the streaked brown hair and the shaky fingers scraping through it in the panicky gesture she often used when she needed something from him. His defenses immediately sprang up.

"I've been looking all over for you." She spoke with a quiet, worried voice. Taking off her glasses, she revealed a pair of weary brown eyes with dark, moist smudges beneath them, and he knew she'd been crying again. "I looked at the studio, at the apartment . . ."

Damn it, he thought. If she just wouldn't *cry*. . . . He tried to keep his defenses up, but her tears always managed to make them slip. "So you found me," he said. "When did you get here?"

"A little while ago." She reached for his drink, sipped, then discarded it with a grimace. Shoving back the brown-gold crimps of hair that set her image somewhere between *Vogue* model and rock 'n' roll junkie, she gazed up at him with liquid eyes. "Doug, you've got to help me. You're the only one who ever could. The only one."

As they always did, her tears erased the speech he'd prepared for her, the animosity that ate at him when she wasn't there, the weariness over the same old argument, and he felt himself wanting to try to explain his side again so she could understand it this time. A man didn't turn his back on a woman in trouble, and he didn't kick dirt in her face when she was down. He stood up and set his arm on her shoulders and pulled her to a corner table. "Come on, Trish," he whispered. "Let's talk. It can't be that bad."

But something inside reminded him that, with Trish, it always was.

An hour later Marti got off the bus in front of the Unicorn lodge and stood on the sidewalk, reluctant to go back to her small, lonely apartment. Somberly, she leaned on her crutch and went into the lodge.

The Pegasus, she thought. She would go there. After all, she should get to know it better if she'd be booking entertainment there. She could get a cup of hot cocoa and think and bury herself in the end-of-day ski crowd lingering over for happy hour.

The bar was dark and disappointingly empty. She pulled onto a stool at the bar and propped her crutch against another, then shed her coat. Pivoting, she glanced at the large television screen on the wall, with videos of classic "wipe-outs" shot on the slopes the day before. Smirking, she thought how they would have loved to have filmed hers.

A couple in a dark corner caught her eye, and she glanced toward them. A woman with crimped hair striped brown and gold and piled almost elegantly sat with her back to Marti as she pressed a kiss on the man's lips. Distractedly, the man's eyes moved up, drifted past Marti, then screeched back.

And Marti's heart fell when she realized that the man was Doug.

The bartender asked what he could get her, but

Marti ignored him. A man gave her a leering grin, but she rebuffed him. Grabbing her coat, she stuffed it under her arm and stood up. Practically dragging her crutch behind her, she limped out, disregarding the pain in her foot and knee as she walked. All she wanted was to get out of Doug's sight and force herself to realize that her question to him had been answered. He *was* involved with Trish Tanner.

And she had no idea why the sight of them together had cut her so painfully, and why she had absolutely no control over the new feelings plaguing her.

CHAPTER SIX

Control comes in many forms, and that evening Marti found it. "Amazing," Amanda exclaimed as she stood watching Marti sitting on the floor amid a mane of wires and cords that tangled to her stereo, her tape deck, and her television. "How did you do that?"

Marti adjusted the volume on her receiver and saw that it was, indeed, picking up the television station in "stereoplex" sound. "Ignorance, I think. I don't know enough about this stuff to know whether it'll electrocute me or not."

"But you didn't even read the instructions."

"I never read instructions. That's why I have a sprained ankle."

Marti grinned up at her old college friend who had suggested she come here to this single's paradise to start over. Amanda's brown bob haircut made her look like a seventeen-year-old high school junior rather than a twenty-eight-year-old barmaid. "It's simple. It just takes common sense. If there's a hole with nothing in it, and a plug that isn't plugged, voilà. The two probably go together. And if they don't, you just swap out a little."

Amanda messed up her hair and finger-brushed it

back into place. "Then you just operate on the principle 'whatever works'?"

"Exactly."

"You know, that principle could work with men too. I could have gotten one of the guys at work to do that for you. Or you could have gotten that guy who took care of you. It won't kill you to admit you need a little help."

Marti dusted off her hands and pulled the rubber band out of her hair, absently beginning to work it out of its French braid. "I *don't* need help. You just watched me do it myself." When her hair was loose she turned off the television and switched on the radio, smiling when the FM station blared to life.

Amanda went for Marti's abandoned sandwich and french fries that sat cold on a plate on the coffee table. "I'm not just talking about the stereo. I just mean that if that guy Doug was helping to get your mind off of Mike, then seeing him was a good idea."

Marti curled onto the couch and propped up her foot. "Yeah? And who's going to get my mind off of Doug when it all blows up in my face? It could turn into a never-ending cycle. He's rich, you know. Drives a Porsche and lives in a condo that's worth a fortune. Just like Mike. History is already repeating itself."

"Horrible," Amanda commiserated as she chewed on a french fry and studied her friend. "It must be awful to attract only rich, handsome men. I'm lucky. I always wind up with ordinary guys who make their lift-ticket money shoveling snow." She took another bite and shook her head. "Look at you. You're gorgeous. I'd cut off an arm for the hair alone. Would you believe that four men who work with me and saw you this morning asked me if I'd introduce them to you? And I've had a severe crush on one of them for the past two months!"

"He's all yours," Marti said. "I'm not interested."

"What are you gonna do? Evaluate every man's financial status and go out only with the ones who qualify for food stamps? Just sit here and mope? Mike owes *you* penance, Marti, not the other way around. You owe it to yourself to get into the swing of things. And you don't do that by hiding inside this apartment and hooking up your own stereo."

Marti found her friend's grim picture of her amusing. "Aren't you overdoing it a little? You act like hooking up my stereo could have been a major social event and I blew it. I've only been here a few days. The first day I moved in, the second I nearly died, and on the third I started a job that looks like it's going to be pretty stressful. Tonight I'm resting. What would you be doing?"

"I'd be at the Pegasus meeting some of those nice guys who are dying to meet you."

"Maybe another time," Marti said. "I'm just tired. Besides, I was at the Pegasus earlier. Once a day is enough. It was a long night the other night, and I haven't caught up—"

"That's another thing!" Amanda interrupted, stopping her with a wagging french fry. "That night. You spent the entire night with a man who did nothing but take care of you, and you don't even want to talk about him now. Don't you think something's wrong with that?"

"Not when he's already involved with someone." She hadn't told Amanda who that someone was, but the woman's name somehow made the situation much less tolerable. "I'm not interested in becoming the 'other woman.' That role doesn't suit me."

"Then what role does? Victim?"

Marti stiffened a degree and dropped her foot. She was rapidly growing tired of this conversation. "I don't much like the sound of that, either. I prefer to think of myself as a survivor. So I have a few scars, maybe, but hopefully they've made me tougher." She sighed and sat back. "And smarter."

Amanda marched to the patio doors and drew open the drapes in an almost violent motion. A portrait of snow-flurried night filled the glass doors, and the moon vaguely outlined the peaks jutting in the distance. "Look at that," Amanda said, tapping on the glass. "This is Breckenridge. People come here to breathe. To be free. To meet other people. To be happy."

"Maybe it's the altitude," Marti said, as if that had some relevance to the emptiness within her.

"Maybe it's the altitude," Amanda mocked in an unflattering voice. "And maybe it's cowardice, and maybe it's—"

The doorbell rang, and Amanda's eyes brightened with hope as she let her insights hang. "Expecting someone?"

"No one." Marti got up and limped to the door. Doug burst in like a diver who knew he couldn't be called back once he plunged in headfirst, before she had the chance to say "Hello," bringing with him the scent of two-hundred-dollar-an-ounce after-shave. He looked around quickly as he sanded his hands together. "No fire? It's freezing out there."

Marti cast an embarrassed look toward Amanda, who grinned like a fourth grader who'd just successfully recited the Preamble to the Constitution. "Amanda, this is Doug Duziak. . . ."

"Nice to meet you." He reached for her hand, shook it rapidly, as if any lull in his momentum would give Marti the chance to throw him out. Then he strode to the glass doors and looked out to Marti's balcony. "Good. At least you have some wood. I'll start you a fire."

Marti felt her tenuous control deteriorating again. "Doug, if I wanted a fire, I'd start one."

"The logs are heavy," he said, nodding toward her ankle. Giving a sue-me shrug, he opened the glass doors and disappeared into the darkness.

"Cute," Amanda whispered. She grabbed her jacket and started pulling it on.

"Don't you dare leave me here!" Marti told her. "Help me get rid of him."

Amanda gave her an it's-for-your-own-good wink. "If you think you need to get rid of him, then you obviously have no conception of what's good for you. I'm leaving."

Doug came back in with an armload of firewood and dropped the logs on the iron grid inside the fireplace. If he could just keep moving, he told himself, keep things hopping, she wouldn't have time to react. He glanced up and noticed that Amanda was zipping her coat. "I'm not running you off, am I?" *Thank you,* his smiling eyes told her.

Amanda bit back her smile and nodded a silent "You're welcome," then started for the door. "No. I was just on my way to the Pegasus. Marti didn't want to go, so . . ."

Marti opened the door and gave Amanda a razor-sharp look as she started over the threshold.

"It was nice to meet you, Doug."

Somehow, the way Amanda grinned and stared at him with distinct purpose in her eyes gave him hope. She *had* heard about him. That was a good sign. And she knew enough to leave them alone. If Marti had been cursing him all afternoon, her friend would have stayed planted in the apartment.

He waved good-bye and looked back to Marti as she closed the door. Her face was blank, unwelcoming, the image of disgust and discomfiture. Doug slipped off his jacket and tossed it onto a chair, as if he'd been there a thousand other times. "How were the slopes?" he asked as he stacked the wood.

"Cold," she said in a voice equally so. She sat down on the arm of the sofa and took a deep breath, preparing to launch a speech. "Doug—"

"Yeah, it must be the coldest day of the year. I love it, though. It's invigorating."

"Doug . . ."

He turned on the gas, lit a match. "You know, the slopes at Keystone are open at night. I'll take you there after work sometime. After your leg is better, of course. It can be—"

"Doug!" Marti stood up, forcing him to shut up. Doug sat down on the raised hearth, his face cloaked in dread, and turned to face her. She was wearing a black sweater with a thin gold chain draped down the front, and her hair, swirling in soft braid-induced waves, looked as if she'd just been coiffed for a model's sensuous photo session. He forced his mind off of his attraction and listened to what she was saying. "Doug, you don't have to come over here and start my fire, and you don't have to take me to Keystone, and you don't have to keep me company. I don't want to see you. I thought I made that clear today."

He moved to a stuffed chair and leaned back, insouciantly clasping his hands behind his head. "You look great in black," he said softly.

She groaned and stepped toward him, reminding herself that the very charm that attracted her should also keep her away. "It won't work, Doug. Please. I don't want you here."

An old favorite song began playing on the radio, setting a mood that she was determined not to feel. But Doug's determination was equally strong.

His eyes lost their evasion glaze, and he leaned forward, setting his elbows on his knees, and looked at her with eyes so green and riveting that she wished that things could be different.

"Marti, just talk to me. Just listen. And then I'll leave. I have to be at work in an hour, anyway."

The limited time span made things seem a little less volatile, so she nodded with slight resignation and sat down on the couch. He got up and moved next to her. For the first time that night she noticed that he wore a burgundy cashmere sweater with a cotton shirt underneath. The colors brightened his eyes and the bronze of his skin, and made him even more undeniably attractive.

"I like you, Marti. The other night something happened while you were sleeping. I felt good. Just looking at you made me care about something again. And I had believed that I'd go on being numb."

She closed her eyes. If only he didn't hit so close to home when he spoke, she thought dolefully. "All right," Marti conceded, opening her eyes and stroking her fingers through her hair in a slow, nervous gesture. "There was some chemistry there. But that's all."

"No," he whispered. He set his elbow on the back of the couch and leaned his head on his fist. "I've felt chemistry before, although I usually call it lust." Marti's cheeks reddened, and she dipped her head. "It wasn't just that." He waited for her to bring those startlingly bright eyes back to him before he went on. "It's Trish that's got you pulling back, isn't it?"

She met his eyes, honestly this time. "I don't like invading someone else's territory. I'm not that kind of person." The contempt in her voice told him she had encountered that type person before.

"I'm not Trish's territory." He rubbed his forehead and sighed. "All right. I'll be honest. I've known Trish since we were teenagers. We had a thing going back then, but we weren't really compatible. We had different values, different dreams. After a while it all fell apart. We haven't been lovers for about eight years now. We've always been close friends, though." The last line made him wearier, and he closed his eyes.

Marti wasn't buying. "Doug, I saw you with her in the Pegasus tonight. I saw you kissing her. You don't sit in dark corners and kiss women who don't mean anything to you."

"*She* kissed *me,*" he said. "She was upset. She's exhausted from her tour and she's going through a bad time. And she does mean something to me. Like a sister would. I can't just turn my back on her when she needs me."

Marti looked out the window. "I'm not asking you to," she said. "It's just that I don't want to be another tangle in an already established relationship. And frankly, I find it hard to believe that anyone could think of the glamorous Trish Tanner as a sister."

Doug cupped her chin and made her look at him. "I looked up in that bar tonight and saw you looking at me, and I wanted to jerk loose of her, despite her dilemma, despite how she was crying, despite how she needed me, and go to you. If I cared for her, do you think I'd feel that way?"

Marti sighed heavily. "What about Trish? Don't you think she might see things differently?"

He laughed then. "Trish has left a string of broken hearts from Greenwich Village to Beverly Hills. *She* dumped Warren Beatty. Believe me, she gets around. She's not in love with me."

"Yet she comes to you when she's upset? Flies all the way to Breckenridge to cry on your shoulder?"

He glanced out the glass doors and sighed, as if he could never make her understand. "Sometimes."

"Where is she now?"

"She has a condo of her own right outside of town." He shifted on the couch and looked at her again, and his voice fell to a husky pitch. "I told her I had plans with a gorgeous blonde tonight and sent her home, hoping that the gorgeous blonde wouldn't brush me off the way she did earlier. I was devastated, you know."

His smile told her he had survived. Marti couldn't help answering it grudgingly. "It's just that I've been

91

through this triangle stuff before. I can't live with it. And you were so evasive when I asked you—"

"It wasn't you, or the subject. It was my innate defense mechanisms, that always spring up when I feel someone getting curious about me. I've been that way since I was a kid. It's a survival mechanism, because people who seem to care usually don't, and they use whatever they learn as ammunition. As soon as I did it I knew you weren't one of them, but by then you were on your way home."

One of them. Marti refrained from asking who "they" were. "It's not just that, Doug. It's . . . your position. Your social class. It's way out of my league, and I don't belong there. I don't even want to be there. I have no money, no social position, no glamor whatsoever, no talent—"

"But you're such a great skier," he teased.

"Doug, I'm serious."

"So am I," he said. "If I wanted an upper-echelon glamor girl, I know where to look, okay? It just so happens I've had my fill of them."

She threw up her hands, as if he'd made her point for her. "So you want to try something new? See how the other half lives?"

He closed his eyes. "Believe it or not, Marti, your tax bracket has never crossed my mind since I met you. Granted, there may be some deep-seated psychological reason for my attraction to you, but I think it probably has more to do with hormones than money or social class. And as far as glamor is concerned"— he took a handful of her hair and painted the ends across his mouth—"if you aren't the epitome of glamor with those sapphire eyes, and this silky hair, and that way you have of looking at me without really looking at me . . . well, I don't know what is."

Was it his voice that mesmerized her? Or the touch of his fingers in her hair? Or the words that seemed so sincere? It didn't seem to matter at the moment. What mattered was that she felt her choices slipping away, thankfully relieving her of the decision. For she almost believed him.

"So . . . are we okay?" he asked carefully, moving the strand of hair to her own lips. "Are you going to keep running from me?"

His voice imprisoned her heart, and his eyes tamed her soul. "I don't know," she whispered.

"Are you going to run from me tonight?" He feathered her hair across her chin, and his face hovered closer.

"I don't know."

"Are you going to let me kiss you?" he whispered, his breath lighting on her mouth.

"I don't know."

His fingers abandoned the strand and brushed fully through her satin hair as their lips met, and suddenly they both knew that she could not turn away.

She touched his face. His sigh whispered against her throat, and his hands forayed the champagne silk of her hair. His mouth was warm velvet against cold silk, his taste was honey against bitterness, his warmth was sustenance against emptiness.

A million alarms screamed in her system, but instead of stopping her, they urged her forward. He was rebellion, beginning, defiance of all that had hurt her in the past.

He lowered her against the cushions on the sofa, his

weight pressing her deeper. His hands explored soft curves, inhibited by the black sweater that bulked over her, exciting a new yearning, a fluttering tumult of desire that left her breath thin and quick.

Rough, masculine hands stole under her sweater. A carefree abandonment washed over her at his touch, and she acknowledged her need for the feel of his naked chest against her bare breast. But he had been stopped before. His hands glided slowly over her satin stomach, creating new dimensions of arousal as they ventured carefully to the breasts supplicating for his touch. The contact of gentle palm over straining nipple took them to a new threshold, and as if he needed consent to cross it, he broke the breath-starved kiss and looked at her with hooded eyes, opaque with entreaty.

Her eyes answered *Yes . . . yes . . .* as his arousal awoke her own needs. His mouth found hers again, his tongue thrusting with a preview of passion that foretold of the ecstasy to come. But the knowledge that it would be stopped inhibited her.

"You have to work," she breathed, breaking free of his mouth.

A deep groan vibrated against her ear. "Damn session," he whispered. "Supposed to be Gonz's. But Sarah wanted him at their Lamaze class."

His lips lit on her chin as he settled tighter against her, making her dread the moment of parting as she dreaded the end of the world. "Selfish Sarah," she whispered, as if she knew the people of whom he spoke.

"I have to engineer this session." His voice was raspy against her neck.

"When do you have to leave?" she whispered.

He slid up her shirt, and his thumbs circled her steep nipples. "Now."

Their eyes met in stricken expressions, and suddenly they both smiled. "My timing stinks," he said with a heavy, shuddering sigh. "Come with me."

"No. I don't think . . ."

He grimaced as if he couldn't take much more frustration, and pulled her shirt back down. When he pulled off of her she felt a cold shadow in the absence of his weight, and couldn't bear to let him leave her. "Please. Come with me so I won't have to just think about you all night. I'll have you there, and I can concentrate on impressing you as the engineering genius that I am."

She laughed again, a happy sound in the wake of shallow breath. "Won't I get in the way?"

"Well, I'm the boss. If you aren't in my way, I don't see why anyone else would complain. You'll sit in the control room with me. Come on. Come with me."

Marti considered the idea. She was crazy, she told herself. Admitting it was the first step, however. Facing it was the second. Diving in headfirst was the third. And what did she have to lose, after all? Before her mind could shoot out an itemized list, she took the plunge. "All right," she whispered, knowing it probably meant that she was certifiable. "I'll come with you."

The studio was lit in warm colors that splashed on the cloth walls and artificial ceiling, which hid the sound traps behind them. In the center, two guitarists and a bass player recorded the rhythm track, while in two of the adjoining booths were the piano player and drummer. All had a perfect view of the control room, enclosed in soundproof glass panels, where Doug and Reed sat at the console adjusting sound levels, and where Marti sat absorbing the scene with a sense of awe. Just as the song was supposed to be winding down for the last take of the night, the band launched into another chorus, and the vocalist ripped out the lyrics with full force, more for fun than sound.

"Uh, hey guys," Doug said, leaning over the console and pushing a button that allowed him to speak to the group via the headsets each of them wore. The singer only grinned and stripped the headset off, letting it curl around his neck, and kept the rhythm going as the musicians let loose in battle to outdo each other. "Hey!" Doug shouted with a grin that acknowledged his loss of control. He threw up his hands. "Does anybody out there hear me?"

Although the band did, they ignored him completely and continued jamming, satisfied grins relaxing the faces that had been so steeped in concentration until now.

Doug turned to Marti and shook his head. "They always rebel when I've worked them this hard. Guess it's time for drastic measures. Hand me the hat, will you?"

"Oh, no!" came Reed's exaggerated cry. "Not the hat!"

Laughing, Marti looked where he was pointing and reached for the white fireman's hat that decorated the top of the small safe she leaned against. She handed the hat to Doug, and he flicked on it's flashing red light, which lit up the studio in rolling, flaring color.

Setting it on his head, Doug sat back, hands clasped over his stomach, watching patiently as the laughing musicians finally gave him their attention. When the music had dwindled down to nothing, the vocalist rolled his eyes and put his headset back on.

"Welcome back," Doug said with a wave. "Thought I'd lost you. You know, you're paying me by the hour."

"That's it for me," the vocalist said in quick answer to the subtle reminder, inspiring laughter all over the studio. He took off his headset and mouthed that he was ready to call it a night.

"I'll start mixing tomorrow," Doug told them.

Marti noted the camaraderie among the group as Doug got them packed up and out the doors, and she saw the enthusiasm with which he approached his job, even though he had jokingly cursed his other engineer several times throughout the session for having a pregnant wife who needed him. The fact that he never forgot her, sitting quietly in the corner, the subtle winks and the way he reached over from time to time and squeezed her knee, and the times she thought he was concentrating on his work, only to notice later that he was merely watching her reflection in the glass, made her feel more special than Mike had made her feel the entire time she'd known him.

It seemed hours later before Doug finally got the crew to leave them there alone. Then he came back to Marti and sat down in the chair across from her, a cigarette in his mouth. "So, what'd you think?"

"It's exciting," she admitted. "Watching it all unfold from a raw piece into something that can make you tap your feet."

"I knew you'd like it." He got out of his chair and stooped in front of the safe beside her, opened it, and pulled out a tape. "This is my favorite tape that came out of this studio," he said almost reverently as he turned back to the recorder. "I keep it in my safe because I like to listen to it and remember my standards here. It represents perfection to me." Snapping the large spool on to the reel lock, he threaded the tape on to the take-up reel, went back to his toy rack, and pushed a button. Then, taking the cigarette from his lips, he leaned back.

The voice of a young man he had only recently discovered played a song that embraced the very heart of the listener.

"It's beautiful," she said.

He stubbed his cigarette into an ashtray and stood up, took her hand, and pulled her to her feet. *"You're* beautiful."

He reached behind her and dimmed the lights, leaving the soft lighting in the studio to bathe the control room in red-gold hues. His arms came around her, and he swayed gently to the seductive melody, dancing without making her move on her ankle. It was more an embrace than a dance, she thought as she closed her eyes and felt his breath warm in her hair. It was more than sexual. More than lustful. It was almost as if they were in love.

He knew how to create a fantasy, she told herself, even as she let herself play a part in it. He knew how to mesmerize. He knew how to revive passion that she thought had been snuffed when they'd had to stop earlier to come to the studio.

His lips nuzzled her face to his, then closed over

hers. Their tongues met lightly, softly. His arms held her tighter. And she became weaker. . . .

The door to the control room opened suddenly, and they both looked toward it.

Trish Tanner stepped inside and, with the flick of a switch, flooded the room with light, and stood before them with her haughty chin lifted in the air, and murderous, accusing eyes leveled on Marti.

CHAPTER SEVEN

"Trish." Doug's voice came like a verdict across the small room.

"I see I interrupted something." Marti wasn't sure if the hoarse words were designed to intimidate her as much as Trish's glossy leather jumpsuit and the hair that looked as if it had just come from a tumble in bed with some Casanova. Her deep neckline drew the eye to her ample breasts, just below the sparkling emerald that was centered on her chest. "I hope it wasn't anything important."

Doug dropped his stiff arms, and Marti stepped back as if she'd been caught with someone else's man. The guilty feeling enraged her. "What is it, Trish?" Doug asked coldly.

"I needed to talk to you." How did she stand there with such proprietorship, with such cool confidence, even while she looked at Doug like a helpless, devastated child?

"We talked today," Doug said. "I thought I made myself clear."

"You said you'd think about it," Trish pressed. Was that a shiver of worry in her voice?

"I did. The answer is still no."

Marti felt as if she were eavesdropping on a domestic squabble and, grinding her teeth, she sat back down and focused her eyes on the tape running out of music.

Trish stepped farther into the room, touching her forehead with a hand that was suddenly trembling. Her eyes focused on the ceiling, as if she were desperately struggling to hold back her tears. "Doug . . . can we talk for just a minute? Please?" She threw Marti a disgruntled look. "In private?"

The crack in her already hoarse voice made him turn around, and his eyes were suddenly softer at the sight of the sliver of tears in her eyes. He glanced at Marti, who sat rigid in the chair, and she opened her mouth to tell him to talk to Trish and put them all out of their misery. "I could go outside and—"

"No," Doug said. "If Trish wants to talk in private, we can talk in the studio." He picked the tape up and handed it to Marti. "Put this back in the safe for me, okay? We'll go home in a minute." Then he dropped a soft kiss on her lips, making his feelings for her absolutely clear to the woman who waited for him with tears in her eyes. But the exhibition made Marti unbearably uncomfortable.

Doug pushed past her and closed the door to the control room. The whole situation was beyond absurd. Doug had told her he and Trish weren't lovers. And she wanted desperately to believe him. But . . .

Was this how it had started with Mike? Had he succumbed to that same chemistry with the woman she'd found him with? Was Marti now playing the role of the other woman, like the one who had destroyed her engagement? Had Mike lied to the other woman and told her that it was over with him and Marti, then forgotten to tell *her?* Had *Doug* lied?

Too proud to watch them through the glass, she took the big tape off her lap and stooped down to put it into the open safe, in the slot between a few other tapes. A stack of sheet music in the corner caught her eye, and she glanced absently down at it. "Fireworks and Roses," her favorite song, coincidentally Trish Tanner's first hit, lay on the top of the stack, hand-scrawled musical notes all over it, and handwritten lyrics and scratchings below the staff. She slid the stack closer to her and recognized the curling way Doug made the tails of the eighth notes, the slanted way he positioned his accidentals, the sloppy scrawl of his notations and lyrics. The lyrics were scratched through and rewritten, but still they weren't the polished lyrics that Marti had known fluently years ago.

She turned to the second sheet and saw that it was an even rougher version of the song. Quickly she scanned three more versions of the same song and the various drafts of two other of Trish's hits and found that the earliest drafts of each bore Doug's name in the upper right corner. Drawing her brows together, she read over the lyrics and saw that the voice of the song was a man's as he mourned the passing of his feelings for the woman he was supposed to love. Flipping back to the most polished version, she saw that the lines had been changed to fit a woman singer. Why would Trish write a song originally in a man's voice when she recorded it herself? she wondered. And why did Doug have it locked in his safe? Had he helped her with the arrangement? And if their relationship was only friendship, why did he keep Trish's songs and not any of his other clients'?

Feeling suddenly as if she'd stumbled onto something she hadn't been supposed to find, Marti shoved the stack back to its corner and closed the safe. It didn't make sense, she thought. But it wasn't her business.

She pulled back up to her chair and looked through the window to the studio. Trish was clutching his sweater, looking up at him with a pleading face, crying like a jilted lover. She saw him close his eyes and mutter something that only made Trish drop her face against his shirt. When he finally slid his arms around her and held her, Marti looked away.

She didn't want to see the ties that bound them, through a past affair, through the evolution of three songs that had made Trish's career, through years of friendship that no one else could ever erase, through the series of rocky relationships that either of them might try with someone else.

Marti didn't have the strength to fight that kind of bond, and she was determined not to become another tangle in it.

Their ride home was quiet, Doug lost in his thoughts, Marti lost in the dreadful feeling that had come over her when she'd seen him holding Trish again. She thought about the way Trish's makeup ran down her cheeks when Doug finally sent her on her way. And she thought about the hatred in her eyes when she'd looked at Marti, as if she had been the weapon that had destroyed her relationship with Doug. It made Marti angry—more at herself than

Doug—because she knew with all her mind that she had no place in Doug's life.

Doug pulled into the parking lot in front of their condominiums and got out, reaching Marti's door before she had the chance to open it herself. It was amazing the way he played the nurturing role of male so well in a world where that was diminishing. Mike would have laughed if she'd ever suggested such a thing. With a mental groan, she rebuked herself for once again comparing the two men and finding Doug to be on top, despite how she needed to convince herself the two were exactly alike.

Quietly, he set his hand on her back and walked her to her apartment. He watched as she found her keys and opened the door.

"I'm really tired," she said when they were inside. She shrugged off her coat and laid it on a chair. "I think we both are. You'd better go home."

He looked down at his shoes and made no move to go. "I know what you're thinking, Marti. You're thinking that there's still something there with Trish and me."

Marti laid her crutch against a wall and stared at it, as if doing so would keep her from being enchanted by Doug again. "It doesn't really matter what I'm thinking, Doug."

"Of course it does. We were getting somewhere tonight. You know we were."

What was the use in denying it? "You're good with fantasies. I guess in your line of work, you'd have to be. I'm awake now. I can face reality."

"Reality? What reality?"

"The reality that you and Trish have a very complex

relationship. I don't want to be caught up in it. I've already made that clear to you."

Doug unzipped his bomber jacket, then dropped to the sofa and rubbed his forehead roughly. After a moment he pulled a cigarette out of the pack in his pocket, stared at it. "I told you earlier tonight where I stood with Trish. You said you believed me." He set the cigarette in his mouth and pulled out his lighter, which he seemed to regard intently. "Okay. So she came to the studio tonight. She was falling apart, which is not unusual for her. As usual, I couldn't seem to throw her out when she's crying like she's at her wit's end. She's had a rough life, and I feel sorry for her. I owe her. She's done a lot for my studio. She's made me a lot of money by recording there, and she's sent me dozens of musicians who have also made me a lot of money. I can't just turn my back on her when she's going through a crisis." He breathed a laugh and waved his cigarette in the air. "Granted, she's *always* going through a crisis. But how do you discriminate between a really bad crisis and a not-so-bad one?"

"Then it all boils down to money and her connections?"

Doug looked at her squarely, irritation ebbing in his eyes. "Of course not. It boils down to friendship and gratitude." He lit his cigarette and leaned back. "And what the hell? Yes, it might have something to do with money. My studio is my life. She's done a lot for it, as my friend. I've done a lot for her, as her friend. I can't kick her in the teeth just because she's a pain sometimes."

Marti sat down across from him and looked down at her foot, suddenly feeling very tired. "It sounds like a problem. One that you'll have to work out with Trish. It has nothing to do with me."

"So what are you saying?" He leaned forward, his green eyes cutting through the barriers and igniting an aching in Marti's heart.

"I'm saying that I don't think—"

"Don't." He cut her off mid-sentence and got up. In two steps he was in front of her, his hands on her shoulders, looking down at her with eyes that brooked no denial. "Don't say that you don't want to see me anymore. Not after what's happened between us tonight."

Marti spun away from him. "Doug, nothing should have happened between us tonight. It was wrong. I'm vulnerable right now. You represent a bit of rebellion for me, maybe a little revenge. And heaven knows what I represent to you. We can't start something using each other as symbols of what we really want."

"Symbols?" Doug's voice lowered when she expected it to rise, and he stepped behind her, set his hands on her hips, pressed his face into her hair. She closed her eyes. "You want to know what I thought the first time I saw you? You were unloading your car, and I was sitting out on my balcony. I saw your long hair sweeping across your hips, and the high-heeled cowboy boots that made your hips swivel when you walked, and the way you laughed when your friend said something. You were a breath of sunshine, and I wanted to know you. Not some symbol." His arms slid around her stomach, pulled her back against him, as his voice created another fantasy. "The next morning I was getting ready to go to bed after an all-night session, and I saw you outside waiting for the shuttle bus, skis in hand. I decided to sleep later so I could catch up with you and meet you. I wasn't chasing a symbol. I was chasing the most beautiful woman I've ever seen."

Marti stiffened instantly and turned to face him, stepping out of his embrace. "You didn't even know me."

"I know you now," he said softly.

"No you don't." She thought of the jewels on Trish's ears, and the Porsche in the parking lot downstairs. She thought of the sexy photographs on the cover of her albums, and the man Trish turned to when she was in trouble. And then she thought of her own station in life—nobody, with nothing, as Mike had reminded her when she caught him with his rich lover, someone who had more "in common" with him. And she knew she could never compete. "I want you to go, Doug."

"I'm not going," he insisted.

She stepped back and tried to harden herself. "I mean it."

"So do I."

She stared at him for a moment, like a chess player who refuses to acknowledge a checkmate. "How many times do I have to tell you, Doug? We weren't meant for each other. I don't even want to try to make it work. I want out now. Don't make it harder than it should be."

"I'll make it damned hard," he vowed, "if you think you're going to dismiss me just like that."

"What do I have to do to convince you?" she shouted on a wave of frustration. "What is it you want from me?"

"The truth, instead of this symbol crap." He took off his coat and dropped it on a chair, as if to say he was staying. "I want you to admit what we had going earlier tonight. I want you to remember what was happening *before* Trish walked into the studio. What might have happened if she hadn't."

A bitter laugh tore out of her throat. "Is that what this is about? Sex? Are you mad because you didn't get to finish what you started?"

The first anger she had ever seen in him flashed in his eyes and he grabbed her arms. "Lady, if I'd been that determined to make love with you, I *would* have finished what I started. I don't remember an awful lot of resistance from you."

She gritted her teeth and tried to wrench her arms free. "You're too persistent, Doug. You don't hear the word *no.*"

"I didn't hear it because you didn't say it!"

"It wouldn't have done any good," she groped, knowing her argument was getting less and less rational.

"You didn't say it because you didn't want to!" he yelled. "You wanted me here whether you could admit it to yourself or not! Just like I wanted to be here!"

With a great effort, she shook free of him and shoved her hair out of her face, deciding it was pointless to deny it again. "But I don't want a one-night stand. I can't live with that!"

"Neither do I! What makes you think we're so different?"

Her ire was rising with her volume. "Because it isn't just us. It's you and Trish and me. I can't compete with a woman that millions of men fantasize over. I can't compete with a woman who jilted Warren Beatty. I can't compete with a woman who has a diamond on her ear that's worth more than my car! I'm Marti Jackson from Desitin, Florida. Nobody!"

"Who says you have to compete? I told you over and over that there is nothing between Trish and me!"

"Nothing?" She was shaking now, about to fall apart, and determined not to. "You practically have the Trish Tanner archives in your safe! You call that nothing?"

The anger drained from his face, and a stunned look replaced it. "What are you talking about?"

"Her songs, Doug! I saw all the versions of her songs when I was putting the tape back in your safe. The biggest hits of her career locked safely away in *your* safe, with your handwriting, and your name on the arrangements. You helped her with those, didn't you, and they made her famous. I can't compete with her memories and her gratitude, and all the things you two have between you."

She saw him stiffen, saw his hands clench into fists, saw the vein in his temple throbbing. "You looked through my safe? How could you do that?"

The accusation in his voice hurt worse than anything else that had been said. Lifting her chin and swallowing back the pain in her voice, she said, "You told me to put the tape back, so I did. I was trying not to watch the little scene between you and Trish. I found the songs, put them back, and closed the safe. That was it."

"But it was none of your business," he said, lips tightening. "I asked you to put the tape back, not take inventory of the safe."

Marti gaped at him, astounded.

"What were you looking for, anyway?"

"Nothing!" she bit out. "I just saw them. I wasn't snooping, and I resent your implying that I was!"

"*You* resent it? What the hell do you have to resent? I didn't riffle through your things, did I?"

Marti clenched her fists and warned herself not to fall apart until he was gone. "Get out," she told him finally in a quiet voice that held decibels of fury.

Nodding, as if they'd finally come to some agreement, Doug picked up his jacket, pulled it on, and zipped it up slowly, but with unmistakable finality. Without saying a word, he went to the door. Marti closed her eyes and braced herself as he opened the door, went out into the cold, and pulled it quietly shut behind him, leaving her alone.

Marti left the television on when she went to bed that night, for she couldn't bear the sound of loneliness. She slept in her robe, with heavy knee socks and three quilts, but they did nothing to warm her, for she knew the cold came from inside. It was a terrible thing to feel hope, then have it snatched away.

A tear rolled down her temple, and she stared at the ceiling. What was it about her that made her fall for men who were wrong for her? She'd come from a nice home, with two parents who loved one another, a brother and sister who were her friends. Things had not always been easy. She remembered the struggles they'd had when there was too much rain or not enough, ruining her father's crops, but they had hung together, always believing that things would get better. And they always had. There was no deep-seated event in her life that made her crave punishment. And yet she was continually making the same mistake.

Expectations. It all boiled down to her expectations of people. She had expected Mike to be a nurturing, proud groom, a man she could spend her life with, a man who would love her as if she were the only person on earth. Maybe her stable childhood had misled her into thinking that was how life was. You fell in love, you married, you lived happily ever after. But that naive line of thinking invited heartbreak. Nothing was ever that simple.

Another tear soaked into her hair as she remembered how sick her parents had been to learn of her foiled marriage plans. She smiled sadly at the memory that they had almost been more heartbroken than she. It must be terrible to see your child aching, she thought, and be powerless to help.

A soft sob choked from her throat, and she turned over and buried her face in the pillow. Doug had been so angry when he left, she was certain he'd never speak to her again. And that was just as well, because after the judgment in his eyes—as if she'd broken into his house and stolen his silver—she had been hurt too deeply to forget. And she never wanted to see him again, either.

The Cable News Network chattered nonstop about wars and terrorists and a man in Cleveland who'd just turned one hundred, while Marti Jackson cried her heart out in the cold, lonely confines of her empty bedroom.

The ski report spoke of five inches of snow expected during the night, temperatures of twenty below zero,

111

and prime skiing conditions the next day. It was too cold for a body to endure, and yet Doug sat out on his balcony, smoking a cigarette and letting flurries of snow sprinkle his shoulders and legs.

He was a fool, he told himself as he watched the blue lights of a television in darkness dancing in the window of Marti's apartment. There he'd been, trying to convince her that they could make a go of it, and the next thing he knew he was so mad at her that he didn't even trust himself. *She didn't do anything!* he told himself. He had *told* her to put the tape back. He had *known* the songs were there. Damn! It wasn't as though she had been looking for something to hold over his head.

She wasn't like Trish. If he'd gone into the same agreement with Marti as he had with Trish years ago, he wouldn't have felt the need to cling to the original pieces of music, in case she ever turned on him. Marti didn't seem capable of that kind of manipulation, but he had seen Trish use it on other people countless times.

Damn! When was he going to figure out that *everyone* wasn't out to get him? When was he going to outgrow those childhood paranoias he'd gleaned from his mother when he'd watched her manager and her fans and her music bleed her for everything she was worth? When would he ever forget the failure his father had been in comparison, the alcohol and drugs that had sustained him until a plane crash laid him mercifully to rest? The world had done that to his family, and he had never forgiven it. Maybe that was why he felt so duty-bound to Trish. She was another victim of the performer's life, and in a way he had helped put her there. It was his responsibility to help her.

But not the way she wanted. He closed his eyes and thought how it must look to Marti. A woman clinging desperately to a man who couldn't turn his back on her. A man who couldn't offer more than superficial words to set her beliefs to rest. An accusation that slashed through the gossamer threads of whatever had been spinning between them—an accusation that was unfounded, unforgivable.

He dropped his cigarette in the snow at his feet and stamped it out, brushed off his hair and shoulders, and went back inside. Shedding his outer clothes, he stood in front of the fire until the feeling came back to his hands and face. He wondered if she was sleeping. He wondered if she was dreaming. He wondered if he had added a new dimension to the sadness he had already seen in her.

He certainly had for himself.

Going upstairs, he sat on the bedspread and picked up the phone. Slowly he dialed the number.

The phone rang once, and she picked it up. "Hello?" The voice was sandy.

"You left your television on, Hot Dog," he whispered.

When she didn't answer he tried again. "Marti, I'm really sorry for getting so mad—"

A click, so quiet that it seemed to mock the significance of the call, cut off his words, leaving him clutching the cold receiver and listening to the detached sound of the dial tone.

Swallowing back the lump in his throat, he returned

the phone to its cradle. It wasn't over, he told himself for comfort. It couldn't be over. He wouldn't let it.

He lay back onto the pillow at the head of his bed and pulled the side of the bedspread over him, lacking the energy or the will even to crawl under the covers. Covering his eyes with his wrist, he tried not to think how it hurt to lose something he'd been so close to finding, something different than he'd ever experienced, something so elusive he might never come close to knowing it again.

And deep into the night, when his mind still groped for answers, he told himself he was better off without her. Men like him were destined to be alone.

CHAPTER EIGHT

Though Marti felt battered and exhausted when the hard light of dawn forced her to get up before her alarm clock had even sounded, her knee and ankle were much better, and she found that she no longer needed her crutch.

She poured herself a cup of coffee and thought back on the phone call last night. Doug had called. He had apologized.

She breathed a deep sigh and jammed a piece of bread into her toaster. Why did she want to forget all the warnings and trust him? Why did she need his companionship when she knew her feelings were probably nothing more significant than substitution? She had geared herself up to share her life with a man. She had planned for it, prepared herself for it, been anxious for it . . . and when it came crashing down she had taken the next person to come along. That was all it was, wasn't it?

The toast popped up, and she stared at it without interest. If that was all it was, then why had she lain awake all night thinking of Doug instead of Mike? When she acknowledged the ache in her heart why did she connect it with the substitute? She had begun to fall for him, for no other reason than she was a fool.

A soft knock on the door cut into her thoughts, and when she didn't respond, it came again, more loudly this time, more demanding.

Setting down her toast and coffee, she limped in her stocking feet to the front door and peered through the tiny peephole. Doug stood outside the door, one hand jammed in the pocket of his leather jacket, the other still banging on the door. Snow swirled around his head, salting his midnight-dark hair, and his shoulders were hunched up to block the bone-chilling wind. A fatigued look of dread mapped his features in dark lines, telling her he had not slept well, either.

The same yearning feeling that she had felt when he'd called last night ached in her again, but it collided with the seething reminder of a cool accusation and a hundred reasons not to let him in. If she did answer the door, she would have to accept his apology, would have to continue with what was turning into a binding relationship, would have to fight falling in love. And today she wasn't sure she could win that fight.

Marti crossed her arms over her chest, backed away from the door, and slid down the foyer wall. She couldn't answer it, couldn't let him in to start things up again and make her even a bigger fool than she'd already admitted to being. She had to learn to deal with the loneliness, to face the emptiness—or to find a way to fill it without depending on someone else.

Mike had been persistent in his effort to patch things up too. And she had almost believed they could work things out. *Almost* hadn't lasted long, however, when she learned he was leaving her door with that despairing slump in his shoulders and hightailing it across town to the other woman he couldn't manage to sacrifice. Marti's choices had been easy with Mike, and she'd made them with a cool head. Why couldn't she feel as determined with Doug?

The rapping on the door finally stopped, and when she gave in to the need to look out the peephole again, she saw that Doug had gone. Somehow the knowledge left her hollow, and despite herself she couldn't help wondering how long it would be before she saw him again.

Eight days. She had avoided him for eight days, making it clear that she wanted nothing to do with him. Doug had tried—tried hard—not to count the days that crept by, but, as if he were on death row marking off the days until the end, he knew exactly how long it had been since he'd seen her. Eight miserable days. He hadn't even known her that long when she'd severed their relationship, he thought as he rode the hospital elevator to the maternity floor. And yet he thought in eight years he would not forget her. He had tried everything. The roses he'd sent had been returned when she refused to sign for them. The note he'd left under her door she had mailed back to him, unopened. She never answered her telephone, and when he tried to catch her at work, he couldn't get past the secretaries in the outer offices. Was it the futility or the loneliness that plagued him more? He wasn't sure, but he told himself there must be some way out of this black hole he'd cast himself into.

Funny, he thought, walking through the antiseptic-white corridors of the hospital. He had never thought

117

of being a father, having a wife, until just lately. And when Gonz had called this morning to tell him he and Sarah had had a boy, he'd almost felt as if their fulfillment emphasized his emptiness.

He reached the windows surrounding the newborn babies just as they were opening the curtains for visiting hours. Reluctantly, he stepped up to the polished plate-glass window separating him from the small room filled with technical equipment and sought out the baby bearing the name Gonzales. An enchanted smile crept across his face at the grace and unharnessed emotion of the subject of his interest. The bright lights of the hospital robbed the atmosphere of a little of the nursery's magic, but not to the proud parents and relatives and friends who cooed at the crying or sleeping or content newborns lined up in a row before them.

Gonz's new son squirmed in his blanket, his face soft and fragile and sleepy, though now and again he opened his eyes and sought out the light. Gonz, his old friend and right arm in the studio, the man who rarely had a serious thought, was a father.

It was the first time Doug could remember envying another man.

The reflected image of Doug's face caught his attention in the glass, and his own wistful expression startled him. It was the same expression he had seen on Marti's face just days ago when she had stood in the empty parking lot, leaning on her crutch, smiling after the curious little boys who had asked about her injuries. Had the emptiness come as a surprise to her too?

Hurried footsteps came up behind him, and a voice dripping with pride exclaimed, "That's my son!" Slapping a hand on Doug's shoulder, Gonz stepped up beside him and pressed his forehead on the glass. "Handsome little devil, isn't he? Spitting image of his dad."

Doug smiled at the pudgy man with kinky black hair and an ungroomed beard and patted him on the back. "You're a lucky man, Gonz."

"Don't I know it," Gonz murmured, a glimmer of wonder coloring his dark eyes.

The two men stood in silence for a long while, gazing at the tiny bundle, who lay oblivious to them. It wasn't so much the child, Doug thought, tilting his head and smiling when the baby sneezed. It was the love he missed, the warmth and wonder of a lifelong companion, the trust and endurance in a relationship that would last through the best and worst of times.

Gonz's in-laws stepped up to the window behind them, admiring their grandchild with shimmering eyes, and Doug stepped back to give them a better view. He wondered if both of Marti's parents were living, if they would approve of him, if he'd ever have the chance to find out. What was happening to him? he asked himself with self-deprecation. The woman didn't even want to read the mail he sent her, much less introduce him to her parents!

He leaned back against the hospital wall and closed his eyes, the soft, black mustache bracketing his lip like a painted scowl. Ah, why did he want so much? Why did he yearn for something he couldn't have?

It was too late for him, he thought. He had let Marti down, and now she was out of his life, denying him the chance to see her or feel her smooth skin beneath his hands. He clenched them both into fists and jammed them into his coat pockets. He wanted to run out into the night and let out a frustrated yell that would shake the summit. He wanted to pull out his hair and hurt more physically than he did emotionally. He wanted to sleep until he was numb again.

A hand on his arm made him open his eyes, and the beautifully sculptured face of Trish Tanner smiled up at him. "You look tired," she said in her raspy voice. "What do you say we stop in and say hello to Sarah, then go get a drink and talk?"

He rubbed his eyes and shook himself back to reality. Was this Trish Tanner, showing concern for *him?* Was she reaching out to give instead of take? Did she really care?

Of course she did, he told himself. They went back a long way, and friends knew when friends were in trouble. Hadn't he always known when she was?

"Good idea," he answered softly, taking her hand.

She wrapped her other hand through his arm and peered up at him with those lazy, seductive eyes. "You can listen to the tapes of my new songs, and see why I need you so badly. Then you'll change your mind."

Doug stopped mid-stride and glared down at her with blatant disbelief. She wasn't reaching out to him, he thought suddenly. She was reaching *for* him. For what she thought he could give her. For what he didn't have.

"Forget it," he mumbled under his breath, barely loud enough for her to hear. Jerking his arm free, he turned around and started back toward the elevators. And he left her standing there behind him, oblivious to the fact that, for once in their relationship, *he* was the one who needed.

* * *

Another week had passed when Marti answered the door one Saturday morning to let Amanda, loaded down with ski equipment, into her apartment.

The grin on her friend's pink face warned her that something was up as she watched her unzip her jacket and shrug out of it. Then, standing at attention with hands clasped in front of her, Amanda launched into a rapid-fire speech. "I was wrong to accuse you of looking in my safe," she blurted quickly before Marti realized what she was saying. "And I owe you an explanation that will make you understand. I'm desperate and miserable and exhausted from trying to get to you. Please, please, please don't keep running from me. Love, Doug." Amanda held up her hand to stem the words she was certain reflected the defensive look on Marti's face. "Last night he came into the Pegasus when I was working and gave me his season lift ticket to deliver that message," she added quickly. "Said to just blurt it out so you couldn't stop me. His *season lift ticket,* Marti! Do you have any idea how badly that man wants to talk to you?"

Marti pulled her fingers through her hair and went to turn up the stereo, as though it could drown out any more messages being smuggled in. "He shouldn't have done it. I don't want to talk to him."

"Why?" Amanda wailed. "What are you afraid of? That you'll fall in love and live happily ever after?"

Marti's laugh was dry and hopeless. "People don't live happily ever after, Amanda. That's a fairy tale." She rubbed at the tension in her temples and assessed her friend, standing over her like a condemning judge. "How did he look?"

"Sort of like a tired, beat-up Apollo. You're really putting him through it, Marti." She cocked her head thoughtfully. "Did he have a beard before?"

Marti's fingertips tingled at the memory of the shaven roughness on his jaw and the silky mustache tickling her face. "No."

"Well, he's just about got one now. You know, men don't shave when they're depressed. It's a rule somewhere, I think."

Marti forbade herself to dwell on Amanda's observation and looked at the skis propped against the wall, desperate to shift the subject off Doug. The fear of skiing held a close second to her fear of relationships. But the thought of staying home on this Saturday, knowing that Doug would probably try to reach her, seemed more dismal than respraining her ankle. "Well, are we going skiing or not?" she asked, springing up with an exaggerated degree of enthusiasm.

Amanda rejoiced. "You mean you've decided to come? You're going to try it again?"

"I told you I was an idiot." Marti went into her bedroom and got out the new ski suit that she had bought on sale after succumbing to Amanda's pressure about "fitting in" in Colorado. "Guess it's just a matter of the lesser of two evils," she said from the bedroom. "If I have to choose my punishment, I'd rather have broken bones than . . ."

Her voice failed, and Amanda didn't push the issue. It didn't take a genius to see that her friend had a broken heart. And it had nothing to do with Mike. Trusting the stereo to drown out her voice, Amanda picked up the phone and dialed the number Doug had forced her to memorize along with his message. "Meet us at the D Lift in an hour," she whispered when he answered. Then she hung up quickly and smiled to herself before Marti came out of her bedroom.

Over an hour later, Marti, bundled in thermal underwear under her pink ski suit and fuzzy earmuffs and fat pink gloves, sat on a wooden rail in front of the ski rack and stared at her skis as if they had eyes and were sneering back at her. Did she dare snap her feet, so recently healed, into those binders again?

She looked down at the trail map clutched in her gloved hand and felt a premonition of doom. "So I went wrong last time by taking a left when I should have taken a right on Peak Nine?"

Amanda, wearing a fake-fur hat that made her head look like a giant dandelion puff, was distracted, as she had been since they'd gotten there, and Marti nudged her.

"Amanda! Start your manhunt later! I'm not going up there until I've memorized the trail I want to follow."

Amanda snapped her attention back to Marti and looked absently at the trail map. "No problem. Just follow the green signs."

"That's what you said last time, and there weren't any! What if we get separated? What if I get lost again?"

"I won't leave you," Amanda mumbled. Again she looked up and squinted as she scanned the crowds heading for the lifts.

Marti stuffed the map in her pocket and eyed her skis again. *I'm bigger than you are,* she told them mentally. *I'm much more intelligent. You're two strips of*

123

wood, and I refuse to be intimidated by you. . . . A
yell ripped her attention to the crowd in front of her as
a man's skis came out from under him and he fell back
into a soft cushion of snow. "That does it," Marti said,
shaking her head adamantly. "I'm not going."

"Of course you are," Amanda countered.

"No, I'm not. Wild horses couldn't get me on those
skis again."

"Uh-huh," Amanda said with an amused smugness
that made Marti regard her suspiciously. Amanda's
eyes had grown wide with recognition, and when she
smiled at someone in the distance, Marti followed her
gaze.

Doug Duziak was walking toward them, clad just
the way he had been the first day she'd met him.

Marti was off the rail in an instant, clicking on her
skis and adjusting her poles to pull herself toward the
lift.

"I thought you said wild horses couldn't drag you,"
Amanda chanted with laughter in her voice.

From the corner of her eye, Marti saw Doug, his
face pale, though just shaven, his green eyes squinting
as he watched her disappear into the crowd lining up
at the lift. The despair in his eyes tugged at her heart,
but it also made her more determined to get away
from him. She was weak . . . too weak. And something about him had left shadows in her heart.

When it was their turn to catch the lift, Amanda
hurried her out, and she held her breath as the chair
scooped her up. It was absurd, her being here again,
she thought. She would probably fall sixty feet off the
lift, or drop one of her skis, or . . . Memories of the
broken lift at Keystone fleeted through her mind, the

way it had snapped like a rubber band and thrown the passengers into the air. She closed her eyes and tried to allay the fear by thinking about something else.

Inevitably, her thoughts went back to Doug. "I wonder if he knew I'd be here," she mumbled.

Amanda looked out over the quiet majesty of the Rockies and dusted the snow off of her legs. "How could he know?"

Marti glanced back over her shoulder to the couple coming up behind them. "Yeah, you're right. He couldn't have known."

She thought about the look on his face, the please-don't-run-away-again expression, and she almost wished she had talked to him. "At least he can't follow us up here, since he gave you his lift ticket and everything."

Amanda's eyes held a secret, smiling sparkle. "At least."

Marti glanced over at her friend, who sat swinging her skis back and forth as the lift took them higher. "Did he really give you a *season* ticket just to get a message to me?"

Amanda stopped fighting her impish grin. "He offered cold cash, but I wanted something more substantial."

Marti couldn't believe it. Why didn't he give up? Why, why, *why* didn't he see that she couldn't cope with this?

"Of course he could buy another ticket if he was determined enough. The money wouldn't be a problem."

Marti closed her eyes and let out a huge sigh. "If I

make it down this slope, I'm going to catch the shuttle and go on back home. I really don't want to see him."

Amanda shrugged as if it was no concern of hers. "Okay, but if you ask me, it seems awfully romantic. I wouldn't mind being in your predicament. Skis up," she reminded Marti as they came to the lift station and their skis touched the ground.

Marti held her breath and sent up a silent prayer as she watched Amanda ski gracefully down the small incline.

"Come on!" she shouted to Marti.

Marti closed her eyes and let the chair dump her. With her skis pigeon-toed and her knees bent, she tumbled into a soft bank of snow and looked up at her friend with eyes both murderous and suicidal. "Some people just aren't cut out for winter sports," she moaned before the people on the next chair lift leapt out of their seats and tripped over her. "I hate this!" she screamed, but it was of no avail. Unless she was injured—which she was determined not to be—there was only one way down.

She hates me, Doug thought as he rode the lift up to where Marti had gotten off. *I've ruined it.* He asked himself why he kept on trying, why he didn't give up, but the answer eluded him. He was crazy—that was why.

When Amanda called this morning she had awakened him on the couch, where he had fallen asleep, too tired and too lonely to go up to bed. An album he had put on last night and set on "repeat" still played, the fire was still burning, and he was still wearing his boots.

Such was the power of this woman, he mused. Until he met Marti he had been a relatively untouchable, self-protective man living in his tiny world where he was sure of the shallow, predictable relationships he had. And this morning when Amanda had called with those nine little words, "Meet us at the D Lift in an hour," he had felt as if his cave had opened up and light was finally finding him. But now, since he had seen her face as she hurried like a spooked doe toward the lift, he knew better.

He came to the end of the lift and stood up at precisely the right time, skiing gracefully to the fork in the road. Amanda would probably have led her down American, he reasoned as he looked at the choice of trails, so he started in that direction. His stomach flip-flopped when he thought how she might hurt herself again, and this time not have him there to help her.

He had to stop that, he told himself as he whisked downhill as fast as he could, looking for the pink ski suit she'd been wearing. This feeling of protectiveness was no good. Hadn't he realized by now that she didn't need or want his help?

He came to a fork in the road that gave the choice of Sundown or Lower American, and trying to use her reasoning, he chose to stay on American. Suddenly he saw her up ahead, clutching her poles as if they were lifelines, her long, silky hair flapping against her back. Amanda had gotten too far ahead of her and stopped, and Marti stood over a steep incline, negotiating her way.

Doug slowed his speed and skied several yards behind her, reluctant to disturb her as she made her way down. Someone needed to work with her on her turns, he thought, and tell her not to wedge her skis so much. Someone needed to—

His thoughts switched into the panic mode as she lost her footing and slipped, starting on a long slide that didn't stop until she hit the bottom of the small hill. He hurried behind her, aching as she tried to reach one of her poles, tried to stand up, slipped, and fell again. He heard her curse and he smiled. Now was the time, he told himself. Now was the time. . . .

Marti cursed again and tried to stand up, but for the life of her she couldn't get her weight directly over her feet before she started sliding again. Why had she tried to do this again? Why?

Someone whisked to a halt beside her, a light spray of snow in the wake of his skis sprinkling her clothes, and she looked up. The same dark skier who had rescued her once before stood over her, holding his hand out to help her up, his glasses reflecting the misery in her face.

"You okay?" he asked quietly.

Taking his hand, because she had no other choice, she let him pull her up. "I'm fine."

He took his glasses off as she came up to face him, and she glanced away, desperate not to look into his eyes.

"Marti?" His hold on her hand tightened, and he moved closer to her. "Please talk to me. Please let me explain things to you. You're driving me crazy."

Marti blinked back the mist in her eyes. "Doug, I don't want to talk to you. Don't you understand?"

He dropped her hand and gazed into those eyes, full of azure anguish, and he knew there was more there than she was telling. "No. I don't understand. Make me understand."

She let her shoulders fall and sighed deeply. "I'm sorry," she whispered.

"No, I'm sorry. For the things I said about the safe. You'll never know how sorry."

She held up a hand to stop him. "It wasn't that so much," she said. "It's all the signs. I see it coming again, Doug, and I don't think I can stand it a second time."

"See *what* coming?" he asked.

She looked down the hill at Amanda, who still waited for her, and Doug turned her face back to his. "Marti, look at me. What is it that you think you see coming?"

She looked at him, struggling with the mist glittering in her eyes. "Humiliation. Disappointment. Deception."

"I'm not going to hurt you!"

"No one ever *plans* it!" she returned. "Mike didn't set out to hurt me, either."

A gust of wind whipped around them, and she felt as if Doug's eyes could penetrate into the confines of her soul. "How did he hurt you, Marti?"

She tried to laugh, but the tear dropping down her cheek gave her away. "He had another woman."

"But I'm not like that."

Marti's lips quivered, and she tried to compress them. "You have Trish, Doug. You have money. You have charm. You're just like him."

"I'm not." His hand tightened on her arm, and she tried to pull it away. "Marti, you've got it all wrong. Please don't see him when you look at me."

129

"I don't," she confessed. "When I think of him I see you. And I tell myself that it's all inevitable. I'll repeat this cycle over and over unless I stop it myself. And that's exactly what I have to do." She pulled her arm out of his grip. "I'm sorry," she said again, and then without thinking whether she was capable or not, she took off in the direction Amanda had gone and left him standing there alone.

CHAPTER NINE

Marti sat in her wooden rocker the following night, effectively blocking out the laughter and voices around her as she flipped blankly through a magazine and tried to forget what day it was. *February 23*. Her wedding day.

Amanda, being the dear and well-meaning friend that she was, had decided that Marti needed company to get her mind off "what might have been." So she had surprised her by bringing over two of the men she swore were "dying" to meet her. Biff, the blond—did mothers actually *name* their children Biff?—had led the others in his refusal to be dismissed, declaring in his Malibu accent that he was a professional athlete, and professional athletes didn't give up that easily. The men made themselves at home, propping their feet on the tables and flirting arrogantly with Amanda and her, completely ignoring Marti's brush-off attempts.

Casting a sidelong glance at Biff as he launched into a second-by-second account of his latest downhill win, Marti gulped back a yawn. Drawing her eyes back to the magazine, she pretended to be interested in an article on winter horticulture. Instead, she caught herself thinking of Doug Duziak again. It had been hard skiing away from him yesterday, so hard. Not to mention terrifying. It was funny how one fear diminished another. But somehow she had managed to make it down the mountain without breaking anything, and then she had taken off her skis and come home. But getting him off her mind hadn't been that simple.

Biff stood up to demonstrate the brilliant technique he'd used to win the downhill slalom championship last year, and Marti tried to look interested. If only she could get rid of them and be alone.

The telephone rang, and for the first time in days she answered it without thinking. But the relief in her voice quickly faded when she recognized her ex-fiancé's sleepily seductive voice.

"Hi, babe," he said in that Elvis Presley cadence that used to make her skin break out in goose bumps.

Marti caught her breath and stood up, dropping the phone to clatter on the floor. "I'm . . . just a minute . . ." She picked up the phone and looked awkwardly around at her guests. "I'm going to take this in there," she murmured as she hurried into her bedroom.

Sitting in the dark on the bed, Marti closed her eyes and took a deep breath before she put the phone back to her ear. "What do you want, Mike?"

"I just wondered how you were spending our wedding night," he said in a deep whisper.

She swallowed back the emotion clogging her throat and lifted her chin. "Oh, was that today? Yes, it is the twenty-third, isn't it?"

He didn't answer her for a moment. She could almost see him bristling and hardening those dazzling eyes. "So how's it going up there?"

"It's great," she said too brightly. "I love it here. I've learned to ski. Listen," she said when her voice started to crack, "I can't talk long. I have some friends over."

Again the line was quiet. "I'm not seeing her anymore," he said finally.

She didn't answer. What in the world did he expect her to say?

"I was wondering if maybe I could come up there and see you."

Strangely, she wasn't angered by the suggestion. She was merely surprised. Surprised that it hadn't stirred something deep within her; surprised that it hadn't hurt; surprised that she was no longer weak against him. "What would be the point, Mike?"

He laughed, and she pictured those deceitful lines crinkling at the corners of his eyes. "The point? The point is that we loved each other. That we would have gotten married tonight. That this was the night you'd been saving yourself for all this time." His voice lowered to a husky pitch with the last words.

"Saving myself?" She couldn't believe he still had such nerve. "That turned out to be a colossal joke, in light of the fact that the only thing *you* saved was your availability." Somehow the uttering of it didn't hurt as much as it had over the past few weeks.

"I was weak. And I've paid. Why can't we just start over?"

She laughed—an almost genuine sound, an almost genuine feeling. "Because I don't want to be involved with a weak man, Mike. Because I've gotten along just fine without you. Because I don't have any feelings for you anymore."

"Come on," he blurted without conviction. "You expect me to believe that you've forgotten what we meant to each other?"

"Why not?" she asked through her teeth. "You forgot long before I did."

The pain in his voice sounded authentic, but it only made her angrier. "Marti, it was going to be our *wedding* night. We were supposed to be toasting our future with champagne, and making love, and planning our family—"

"Stop it, Mike," she cut in. She closed her eyes and tried to cool the anger swelling within her.

"But, Marti, I can give you *everything*. Things you've never had!"

"Just stop it. It's over and behind us. I don't want to talk to you again."

"You can't just keep running, you know!" he shouted into the phone. "Sooner or later you'll have to face it."

She stood up, prepared to end this once and for all. "No, *you* face it. You won't see me again. And the next time you get engaged, you remember what's at stake if you feel yourself getting 'weak' and craving other women. Remember that some mistakes can't be corrected with the almighty buck!"

She slammed the phone down, listening to the ring of the impact, and blinked back the tears burning her eyes. She clutched her head and wished those people were out of her house so she could cry her heart out. But they were here, and she couldn't let them hear her fall apart. Quickly she grabbed her coat and pulled it on. Wiping her eyes, she went back into the living room, keeping her face turned away from them. "I have to go out for a little while," she said.

"But we ordered a pizza. If we leave, they won't know where to deliver it," Biff argued.

Marti shrugged. "Stay here. It'll be all right. I just have to go."

The cold night drew her into its darkness like an old friend embracing her. Burying her hands in her coat pocket, she stepped carefully down the snow-covered steps, two inches thick with fresh powder that had accumulated that afternoon. The crescent moon overhead cast a bluish tint to the ground, and the wind whipping around the corners of the complex chilled her to the bone, but the shivering of her limbs did not bother her. All she wanted was to get away, to end this miserable chapter and move on to the next page in her life.

Biting her quivering lip, shaking more from the tears spilling over her lashes than from the cold, Marti went to a tree on the median of the parking lot and leaned against it, using it as a wall against the chilling wind. She was tired. So tired of being the victim. So tired of worrying about doing "the right thing" when it wound up wrong anyway. So tired of hurting.

Closing her eyes and letting the tears burn down her face, she took a deep breath. She had come to a turning point in her life, and the possibilities all seemed dim. Perhaps her relocation had only complicated things more, for now she couldn't get Doug Duziak out of her mind, either.

The distant sound of a strumming guitar caught her ear on the breeze, and wiping her face and turning into the wind, she followed it. It was a melody that could have won battle with the sirens, drawing Marti toward it, soothing her anger and confusion and promising solace and warmth in exchange for the simple task of trusting. As it grew louder with her approach, she knew that it was coming from Doug's balcony.

Stopping cold in her tracks, Marti stood in the middle of the snow-covered parking lot and gazed upward at the balcony, seeing nothing but the live tip of a cigarette against a backdrop of opaque darkness. The music enchanted her, beckoned her, blocking out all thought but that of the face of the man behind it—the face she had awakened to when that tune woke her two weeks ago.

She stood motionless, staring up at the balcony, wondering whether she dared call out to Doug and bask in his comfort just one more time. If she did, she would be responsible for how far this meeting took them. But what did it matter, considering that she always chose the wrong men to love anyway, that she deserved a moment of peace after what Mike had done. This time with Doug wasn't like real life, only a dream that had to be seen through to the end or repeated over and over again. A fantasy that had to be purged.

Before she had made a decision, the music stopped suddenly, and the tiny light of the cigarette made a quick descension from the lips that held it. Some change in the shadows told her Doug had stood up, and she was certain he saw her.

"Marti?" His voice above her was uncertain, soft, beckoning.

"Hi," she said, so low that she doubted he heard. An instant of panic flashed through her mind and she

136

stepped back, contemplating whether to return to the safety of Biff or to follow the flow of the fantasy she seemed to be playing out. The fantasy that was both curse and miracle.

A miracle. She was a miracle standing there in the shadows, Doug thought, long hair rustling around her face like a part of the wind itself. The blue of her eyes was almost distinct against the night as she peered up at him, and the indecision on her face was clear in the moonlight.

"Where did you come from?" he asked, afraid to move to let her in for fear that she would disappear as quickly as she'd come.

"I was just out walking," she said in the sweetest, most vulnerable voice he'd ever heard. "I heard you playing."

"Walking?" he asked. "It's a cold night for a walk."

"It's a cold night to sit outside playing guitar too," she pointed out. "Guess when you need to breathe you forget about the cold."

A moment of quiet connected them in startling intimacy, and finally Doug's voice cut across the wind. "Sometimes it's colder inside than it is out."

"Sometimes," she agreed. She cleared her throat.

Doug's heart lurched at the raw need apparent in her face, and holding out a hand as if to cast a spell that would keep her from leaving, he stepped back. "Wait there. I'll let you in."

"No, I can't," she returned halfheartedly, her eyes beginning to focus on his face. "Some people are waiting." Her voice trailed off when his face fell and his eyes fixed on hers. Setting down his guitar, he leaned over his rail.

"Please, Marti," he entreated softly. "The fire's warm and . . . and I've been thinking about you."

His need touched her more than her own, for she knew he understood the desolation she was feeling. Over and over she had denied him, but now she seemed to have no choice. No choice at all, for she had left her rational side in her apartment with Biff. Nodding acquiescence, she waited while he disappeared into his condo, flicking on a light in the center of the room that cast a yellow glow on Marti until she started for the steps leading to Doug's front door.

He was still wearing his coat when he opened it, and he smelled of wind and smoke, but it was his eyes, so appreciative, so compelling, that moved her. He took her hands in his, numb with cold, and drew her into the warm apartment. "You came," he said, as if he couldn't believe it. "You're here."

"I'm freezing," she said on a nervous breath.

He led her to the fireplace. A soft stereo melody drifted in the air like the score to a film that she was a part of.

When he opened his jacket and shrugged it off, she did the same, handing it to him, watching him toss it onto a chair. He was wearing a green and black flannel shirt, and his nose was pink from the cold. Warming his hands before the fire, blazing up over the logs like protective arms, he looked at her, his eyes two fiery emeralds whose brilliance dazzled her. "Marti, I'm sorry about what I said about your finding the songs. I'm so sorry."

She shook her head and shrugged. "No, I'm sorry for avoiding you. It's been . . . a rough time for me."

She tried to blink back the tears threatening her eyes, and he stepped closer to her.

"I saw two guys go into your condominium a little while ago. It was all I could do to keep from coming over there."

Marti swallowed. "Amanda brought them. She thought they'd cheer me up. She expected it to be a bad night."

"Why?"

Marti took in a breath that sounded like a sob, and Doug reached up to cup her chin. "Tonight was supposed to be my wedding night." She blinked and looked at the ceiling, as if doing so could help her contain her tears. Swallowing, she went on. "Mike, my ex-fiancé, called."

Doug didn't want to hear what she was telling him, that she was hurting over another man. He stepped back, set his elbow on the mantel, and rubbed his forehead.

When a crystal tear escaped her eyes and dropped onto her cheek, Doug breathed a curse and pulled her against him, holding her as if he would protect her from the next pain that hurled itself at her, even if it meant that he would hurt instead. The tenderness in his touch made her tears trickle over. She wrapped her arms around his waist and buried her face in his shirt. She felt his face in her hair, the tension in his embrace, his warm breath as he asked, "Are you still in love with him?"

The question required no thought. Looking up at him, she answered, "No."

He framed her face with his hands, wiped the tears with his thumbs. "Good," he whispered. "Because I want you to fall in love with me. Because I'll never hurt you like that, Marti."

The look in his eyes was soothing, stirring, and she yearned to accept the healing power he promised. His throat moved when he swallowed, and his lips parted, and Marti knew the desperate feeling of floundering out of control as the world spun out from under her.

Slowly his face lowered to hers, and when their lips met the world seemed on course again. His kiss opened doors and shattered walls, and nothing mattered anymore except being with him and accepting the love he had to offer, even if it was just for the night.

His tongue moved in a sensuous dance against hers, testing, probing, drawing feeling that she hadn't known she contained. When he broke the bond of their lips and opened his eyes to her, his breath was heavy, ragged. "What is it about you?" he asked in a hoarse, husky voice. "What is it that makes me want you more than I've ever wanted anyone? What makes me afraid if I touch you I'll scare you away?"

Her glittering eyes opened her soul for full view, and it was futile trying to hide from him. "I'm not going anywhere tonight," she whispered.

The desire in his eyes grew more intense as he tangled his fingers in her hair. Marti raised her own trembling hands and pressed his to her face, holding them there until his lips found hers again.

The touching was as poignant as the kiss itself, as slow and lazy as apprehension required. But the restraint and cruel cadence of their hearts only seemed added parts of the fantasy that Marti intended to see through.

When their lips broke again she willed herself not to melt as his eyes told her secrets, made her promises, inspired the seeds of fantasies she had never dared to imagine. His eyes were saying without words where the evening was leading. And she was in no mood to argue.

The soft music was an aphrodisiac, dazing her as he pressed her so tightly against him that she could feel his desire hammering with fiery frenzy against her. "I've been thinking of holding you this way for more than two weeks," he whispered in her ear.

So caught up were the two in the music of their breath and the rhythm of their hearts that they were not even aware when the songs changed. Doug had danced Marti against the wall, and she lifted her face, hungry for his kiss. His lips hovered above hers for an eternity as he gazed into her hooded eyes. "I could drown in those eyes," he whispered. "And I suspect I will."

He kissed her deeply, and she responded, pulling him closer against her, hearing his breathing quicken when his arms tightened their embrace. His head moved with the force of his growing passion while his lips bared her soul, his tongue moving like velvet against hers, his lower body pressing her against the wall.

Catching his breath, Doug pulled back to look at her, his hands bracing her hips. "My mind tells me to slow down," he rumbled against her lips. "But for the life of me, I can't hold back."

"You don't have to hold back," Marti said in a cracked voice.

Dragging in a long breath, Doug stepped back

enough to study her face with as much objectivity as his heart would allow. "I don't want to hold back," he whispered.

It was Marti who reached out this time, pulling his face down to hers, and kissing him with no inhibitions, no doubts, about what she knew was to come.

CHAPTER TEN

Closing her mind to reason, Marti slid her hands to Doug's back and down to the taut muscles of his buttocks. Her body rocked slowly against his, throbbing with a scorching heat that consumed every thought except that of feeling his skin against hers, exploring the tight beauty of his body, unharnessing the passion that he had carefully drawn to surface within her.

She broke the bond of their lips and rolled her head against the wall as Doug's wet mouth chased across her throat, his hands kneading her hips through the jeans that contoured them.

"Upstairs," he breathed against her neck.

Marti nodded.

Without another word, he pulled her to the winding staircase, and Marti followed him up the steps. The bedroom held a bewitching glow of lamplight, its yellow tone bathing them in warm golden hues. Before Marti had time for second thoughts, Doug was holding her again, kissing her with the truculent force of a starving man. Anxiously, Marti began to work the buttons free from his flannel shirt. Pulling it off his arms, she let it fall to the floor. Her covetous hands forayed the hard muscles of his heaving shoulders and straining biceps as his hands moved her hips against his growing arousal in a rhythm that provoked a deep, frustrated moan.

She ran a shaky hand through the tumble of his hair, her weak legs making her stagger with the raw emotion threatening her. His smoky eyes searched her face for a long, electric moment, offering one final moment to flee, and finally he swept her into his arms and carried her to the bed. Instead of laying her there, he sat her carefully on the edge, kneeling on the floor in front of her, his face level with hers. Maddeningly, he traced one finger along the top edge of her sweater, eyes searing down at the swells of breast that teased him beneath the cloth. Bringing his eyes back to Marti's, he found the front zipper and released it, slowly letting it open. His wet tongue tracing the valley of her breasts robbed her of the last tenets of her sanity. Gentle fingers peeled the bulky knit sweater off of her, revealing the full, tight alabaster breasts against the Florida tan, beckoning him with their erectness. When his tongue painted one brown nipple, Marti gasped against the fire raging through her with each nip of his teeth.

He cast her sweater aside and turned his face back up to her. Grasping the flaxen tumble of her hair, he whispered, "We can stop whenever you want."

We should stop, she told herself. *Too far . . .* But it felt so good, this sense of abandonment. "I'll let you know," Marti whispered without realizing the cruelty of noncommitment. Her hand feathered across his neck, leaving the rough texture of shaven skin, finding the smooth pulse point that hammered at her fingertips. A sigh blew from her lips like a shiver.

He waited as her hands moved across the rounded muscles of his shoulders, down his chest, fingernails scraping lightly over brown nipples nestled in the black sprinkle of hair. His body contracted to every touch, and he swayed against her to encourage more, increasing her pressure with his own.

Finally his wet lips began a trail of passion that awoke every dormant nerve in her body.

"Do you want to stop?" he asked again with trembling patience that belied the hands tracing the waistband of her jeans.

"Do you?" she asked against his lips, the insecurity of the first time clouding her own desire.

"I don't know if I can," he whispered on a breathy laugh, "but I want you to know I'll try if it's what you want."

Her silence caused him to pull back to look at her, his eyes pleading silently for the answer he wanted, the one simple word that could lead her into ecstasy. Her hands moved slowly down his chest, and her eyes followed, fascinated with his beautiful body, thrilled at every muscle that quivered at her touch. Her eyes rose back to his as her hands traversed lower, following the thinning line of hair to his navel. Her finger circled it, and she watched him close his eyes and swallow, his breath suddenly stilled, held captive in his chest. Daringly, she traced the hair below his navel, her own fingers trembling with urgency and need and the slightest fear at something she did not know. As her fingers dipped into the waistband of his jeans, she slid off the bed and knelt in front of him, her mouth suddenly hungry for the taste and texture and feel of his skin. "I want you," she murmured, bringing her lips to his chest, biting his flesh, making him quiver with want as intense as the moan deep in his throat, as all-consuming as his arms closing around her.

Coaxing her lips back to his, Doug kissed her with soul-scourging heat. Her breasts crushed against his chest, his nipples arousing her as much as the hands stealing down her back, sliding into her jeans, taking hold of her hips and pressing her against his own. When her arms closed around his neck he lifted her with him and laid her on the bed beneath him. As if they had rehearsed the ancient ritual, her legs let him nearer, the hard source of his virility cradled urgently against her. The ravishing plunge of his tongue against hers matched the rhythm of their bodies, and Marti yearned to finish the union.

His hands, still between denim and flesh, moved at her hips, and his fingers glided around her. She wanted to scream as he taught her new secrets, wanted to cry as he shared new feelings, wanted to die in his arms and let him revive her to startling new life. Her body arched as his hot breath scaled her breasts. Impatient hands tugged at her jeans and worked them over her hips, sliding them off in one fluid motion. Her body quaked when he stepped from his own and lay above her, his hot flesh melding against hers. His hips poised at hers just before entering, his fingers tested, kneaded, readied her for what she both feared and craved.

Taking her lips in one trembling motion, he entered her slightly, pulled back, entered again, and retreated. His face paled, his eyes glossing over with poignant surprise as her virginity became apparent. She clung to him as he harnessed his movements so as not to frighten or hurt her, and he rocked into her with shivering gentleness, his eyes closing with each new depth he reached. Tenderly, he made his way until the final, burning thrust of consummation.

Then his body moved more forcefully, flying her weightlessly into the summits until she was a part of the clouds, and then the earth crumbled at her feet, dropping her in a final avalanche of passion, falling so fast that she could not find air until she hit a soft bed of warmth that drew her back to lovely, satiated, pulsing reality. Reality so intense, so beautiful, that she cried.

Doug's breath had not found its equilibrium when he lifted enough to look at her, an elbow on either side of her head propping him, while his body still throbbed against hers. "It was your first time," he whispered. "Why didn't you tell me?"

Soft color climbed the crest of her cheekbones, and she smiled through her tears. "I thought you could tell."

"I knew you were an innocent," he told her, stroking the hair out of her eyes. "But I didn't know—"

"It's okay," she cut in. "It was what I wanted."

His hands cupped her face with such tenderness that more tears blurred her sight of him, and his green eyes impaled her as deeply as his body. "But why, Marti? Why me?" His deep voice was probing, moving, inspiring.

After such an honest joining of bodies, there was no room for lies. "Because everything between us has seemed like a dream. And I couldn't really be hurt by a dream, could I?"

His fingers stopped their caressing of her face, and his eyes shaded over with pain.

"I don't want to be just a dream," he whispered. When she didn't answer he pulled up to look at her fully. "So am I revenge or just a new beginning?" His direct question was not posed as a judgment, and it left no room for evasion.

"I don't know," she said. "I just couldn't get you out of my mind, no matter how I tried. It seemed like something I had to play out until the end, to clear it from my head."

"And did you?"

Another tear tumbled into her hair. "No. I don't think making love to you has cleared anything about you from my mind."

"Good," he whispered. "Because the second time is always better than the first." He kissed her then, rekindling her desire, and his voice was soft against her lips. "And the third time is even better than that." She felt his body reviving within her, and when his thumb moved to wipe away her tears, she turned her head and caught it in her mouth. He swallowed and moved deeper inside her. "Trust me, Marti," he whispered on a quivery breath. "I won't hurt you."

"No one ever intends to," she returned.

The naked vulnerability in her face frightened him, for it gave him a responsibility he hadn't been prepared for. But it was one he wanted, for the gift she had just granted him made him feel more protective of her than ever before. His only intention was to wipe the pain from her heart and replace it with love for him. But was that possible? Could a woman like her really find love in her heart for a man like him?

"What kind of fool would hurt a woman like you?" he asked as his tumescence left her gasping.

"It doesn't matter," she said. "I'm not hurting anymore."

He kissed her chin, his body continuing to move deeper. "Good," he whispered. "How *do* you feel?"

"Decadent," she said. "How do I feel to you?"

"Sexy," he breathed. "Maddening. Wonderful."

"Considering my virginity?"

His laughter vibrated against her neck, and he rolled her above him. "Baby, you aren't a virgin anymore. Believe me when I say I've never . . . felt . . . like this. . . ."

Her weight above him gave him more depth, and she felt a thin mist breaking out over her skin. "Doug . . ."

"I love your hair," he moaned as it swept over his face. "I love your mouth. I love your neck. I love your breasts."

Darkness was swimming in her head again, igniting a million tiny lights and the image of a man joining with her in such a binding way that she felt him becoming the very life of her. "Doug . . ."

"I love your skin. I love your taste. . . ."

Marti felt herself folding inside out, swirling and hurling and clinging to him, the one man who made her complete.

And then he rolled her over and took her with him on an adventure that threatened to leave her throbbing, an adventure that would wrench her heart completely from her. But she knew he had given her his in return.

"I'll never hurt you, Marti," he whispered as he

149

trembled against her in the aftermath. "Not for any reason. Not even Trish."

Marti shook her head. It wasn't the time to talk about Trish. "Don't—"

He hushed her with a finger over her mouth. "I have to explain, Marti. Please let me explain."

When she closed her eyes and sighed he pulled onto his side and propped himself on an elbow. "I wrote 'Fireworks and Roses.' Not Trish."

Marti made no response, for she wasn't surprised. It made sense. And now she knew that hearing him say it would reinforce the feeling that she had no place in such a complicated triangle. "Go on," she whispered.

He breathed a great sigh. "Trish and I were . . . involved . . . about ten years ago when she was just starting out. She wrote songs then, but none of them were spectacular. Back then I used to mess around writing songs just for fun, even though I had no desire to do anything with them." He took a curl of Marti's hair and made it into a circle around her breast. "And one day she heard 'Fireworks and Roses' and begged me to let her have it. I felt sorry for her. I knew what a singing career, especially an unsuccessful one, could do to a person, and I wanted to help. I never thought in a million years that song would amount to anything. So I gave it to her, along with the other two you found, and let her take the credit. Nobody was more amazed than I was when all three of them were hits. It was incredible what they did for her career."

Marti pushed his hair out of his eyes. "And you didn't get royalties or recognition or *anything?*"

He shook his head. "All I wanted was to build my studio, and Trish was loyal to me. See, even though

150

the success of the songs was unexpected, I was glad I had helped her, because it was doing something. And all my life I had watched the world chisel away at people who had exceptional talent, and I hadn't been able to do anything. Nothing."

Marti sat up, pulling the sheet modestly with her, and tilted her head. "What do you mean all your life? Had you known Trish that long?"

He rolled to his back and clasped his hands behind his head and gazed up at the ceiling as memories unfolded. "I'm talking about my mother. Both my parents, really, but especially my mother."

Marti sat silent, knowing he needed no prodding.

"Ever heard of Simon Duziak?"

"No," Marti said.

Doug gave a gentle smirk. "That was the problem. No one had heard of him, and *everyone* had heard of Ann Marie Nelson."

Marti was lost. Ruffling her hair in confusion, she said, "She was famous. My parents took me to see her sing once in Tallahassee."

"She was my mother," Doug said, and he watched the surprise taking hold of Marti's face. "And Simon was my father. They both had music careers, and I spent my entire childhood watching it destroy two pretty decent people." He grimaced, the expression telling her this wasn't easy for him. "My mother tried to keep up with the pressures on her, but her managers pushed her so hard that she lived in a constant state of exhaustion and anxiety. And my father was chronically depressed, because as her star rose, his fell." He cleared his throat and went on. "He turned to the bottle, and then drugs . . . and he died when I was about ten."

Marti leaned over him and set her hands on his chest. "Oh, Doug."

He kept his eyes on the ceiling, intent on finishing the purging story, and Marti felt certain that he hadn't shared it with many others. "Mom took me with her on her tours. I had private tutors by day and spent my nights backstage or napping in her dressing rooms. I watched her fall apart piece by piece as the media bled her and her fans drove her and her managers stripped her of everything that made her life worthwhile. And I listened to her cry in bed because her life had gotten out of control, and she'd had to give up so much."

He swallowed and looked up at Marti. "And then when *her* career started heading downhill, I watched it get even worse. Because even though success meant dying a little bit each night, failure was even worse. Performing, being the best, was an addiction to her, and she was terrified of losing it. And the struggle stripped her of all her self-respect, because she would have done anything to get back to where she was. And I was just a helpless kid without any power at all. You have no idea how terrifying it is to see disaster coming and not be able to head it off."

Marti dropped her head to his chest, and he slid his arms around her. "She died several years ago. But emotionally I think she buried herself long before that." He took a deep breath and looked down at the woman in his arms. "Trish and I had more than music in common. She lost both her parents in an accident when she was seven, and a wealthy aunt became her guardian. I was one of the only people who ever cared

152

what happened to her, and I had to help her. She was insecure, and lonely, and the only thing she had in her life was talent that was getting her nowhere. If I couldn't help by talking her out of that career, then I could at least help her to be successful at it. Because I could see her heading on the same course as my father."

"So you thought by giving her three songs you'd be making it easier?"

"It did for a while," he said, "but when she needed new songs she wanted me to write them again. She started to believe that the only reason she had been successful was that I had helped her. She had no faith in her own talent. Still doesn't."

"But she's good," Marti said grudgingly. "Even if I had known someone else wrote her songs, I would have liked her work."

"Of course you would," he said. "But she wanted to be known for doing it all. And she *could* do it all. Some of her own songs made it to the charts. But only the ones I wrote for her reached number one."

She looked up at him, resting her chin on his chest. "Is that what she wants now? For you to write for her again?"

Doug stroked her hair. "She thinks that I can give her career a shot in the arm. It's almost like some kind of superstition with her. I keep telling her I haven't written in years, that I have no interest in trying. But she's convinced that I had the magic touch once and that I could do it again. She just won't let go. And it's hard to shake her off when she's so desperate."

Marti sat up again and looked down at him. "Amanda kept trying to tell me that I didn't owe Mike penance," she said. "He owed me. And yet I've been punishing myself. It's the same with you, Doug. You don't owe your mother penance, and you can't make up for your helplessness with her by always being there for Trish."

He smiled faintly. "You're pretty smart, you know it?" There was a thoughtful pause before he spoke again. "I've tried to cut myself off from her, but I can't seem to do it completely. I'm still drawn to her—maybe by pity, or sympathy, or whatever you want to call it."

"Part of you must like the fact that she needs you," Marti said. "Because maybe you never felt that your mother really did."

He drew his brows together at the rawness of her observation. "Maybe."

Marti felt those barriers rising again. "Is that why you wanted me? Because you found me in a heap on that ski slope? Because I needed you too?"

He sat up, beginning to follow the thread of her thoughts. "No. Well, maybe at first you drew out my protective instincts, but . . ."

Marti rolled to her back and looked up at the ceiling, then back at him. "Even tonight I needed you, when I was hurting over Mike. Is that what draws us together? Some kind of selfish need for each other? Your need to be needed? My need to be protected?"

Doug grabbed her shoulders and made her look at him. "Marti, a person has to feel needed. There's nothing unhealthy about that."

Marti looked down at the sheet clutched to her breast. "Not unless there's someone out there who needs more than you can give. Trish has you by the

154

throat, Doug. She's famous, and sexy, and gorgeous, and she has men lined up at her door, but she keeps coming back to you. She keeps her swimsuit here, she takes baths in your Jacuzzi, she shares the most important moments in her life with you. How can I compete with that?"

"You don't even have to," he said. "Don't you remember the words to 'Fireworks and Roses'? It says fireworks fade and roses wither, but life goes on. I wrote that about my relationship with Trish. She gladly took the song in exchange for my freedom. Trish is not your competition—"

The doorbell chimed, cutting off his words, and Doug breathed a curse. "Who the hell is that?"

It rang again, followed by an insistent knock, and Doug sat up. "Your friend? Is she looking for you?"

Marti looked toward the staircase. "No, Amanda wouldn't come here." The bell chimed again. "You'd better go answer it, Doug."

Irritated, Doug got out of bed and put on his jeans and a shirt. The knocking resumed. "I'm coming!" he shouted.

"We aren't finished with this," he said, turning back to Marti as she reached for her clothes. "Don't get dressed. Just . . . just stay there. . . ." Then, muttering "Damn!" he darted down the stairs.

Marti quickly pulled on her clothes anyway and heard him open the door. She heard muffled, low voices so she walked to the top of the stairs and looked down.

Trish Tanner was standing just inside the foyer, shedding her long sable coat and dropping it to the floor. Marti felt her blood run cold as Trish stripped off her gloves and added them to the pile on the floor.

"Trish, what do you want?"

"To talk to you, Doug," she said. "You ran out on me at the hospital. We were supposed to have drinks."

"I'm busy," he said.

She stepped back and Marti saw the low, daring sweep of her neckline, and the emerald stone sparkling against her chest. Trish grinned up at him and reached out to hook her fingers through the belt loops on his jeans and tugged him closer to her, a gesture meant to be both intimate and seductive. "Busy doing what?"

He pulled her hands off his hips and stepped back. "I have company," he said.

Marti raked her hands through her disheveled hair and made her way down the staircase.

Two startling gold eyes glared up at her, and Trish set her hands on her hips. "Oh, I see."

"Hello again," Marti said as she looked down at Trish in her black leather miniskirt and designer shoes, then back to her own jeans and wrinkled sweater. They were a poor comparison, Marti realized, feeling dowdy and embarrassed.

"Yes, it seems I caught you two indulging once before, didn't I?" The tone of Trish's voice implied that she had some rights to Doug that he did not acknowledge.

Doug didn't like it. "Trish, I don't know why you came here, but—" He was cut off when Trish turned back to him and smiled.

"It's all right. I'm not accustomed to catching you with the same one twice, but I can adjust. After all, we both know that I've had my indulgences over the years."

What was she saying? Marti wondered. That she and Doug had an "open" relationship, when Doug insisted that there was no intimacy between them at all?

Doug opened the door abruptly, and a puff of air came in and swept Trish's hair off her shoulders and into her face. "Trish, go home."

Slowly, with admirable finesse, Trish picked up her gloves and then her sable coat and slung it over her shoulder. "All right," she said, finally. "But all I really wanted to know was whether you wanted us to stay at the Hilton in L.A. again next month. I wanted to go ahead and book the hotel." She touched his mustache and smiled provocatively. "We had so much fun last year."

Doug jerked his face away from her touch and watched as she walked out into the cold. Slamming the door, he turned back to Marti. She already had her coat on, and she was trying to zip it up in short, choppy movements that were slowed by her trembling.

"Marti, don't—"

"Just tell me one thing, Doug," she said, her face stinging. "Did you or did you not have plans to go to L.A. with her next month? Was she just trying to strike out at me or is it true that you went with her just last year when you swore it had been over for eight years?"

"Yes, but you don't—"

She gritted her teeth and pushed past him. "That's all I wanted to know."

"Marti, don't go." His voice behind her was fraught

with need, need that touched her and revealed to her the love she had for him, though she wasn't certain when it had sprung to life. But as it always did, that love caused a fierce aching in her soul that she was desperate to overcome.

Turning back to him with tears in her eyes, she took a determined stance. "I don't need this, Doug. It's my fault, I guess. I must have some kind of psychological problem that makes me keep getting involved with men that I know I should stay away from. Men with secrets. Men with lies. Men with other women. I understand about your lyrics in 'Fireworks and Roses.' I've lived it. They do fade and wither. It's inevitable. Maybe I need professional help. But I don't need you. I don't need any man."

He slammed his hand against the door and stopped her from opening it. "Marti, you aren't walking out on me again! You're going to listen to me."

Marti's reply came on a sob. "Why do you keep at this? Why don't you just find some other side dish to keep you busy? Why don't you leave me alone?"

"Because I love you, damn it!" he shouted. His words echoed through the condominium, penetrating her stunned heart.

She pressed her forehead against the door in defeat, and realized that he had just made it more difficult than ever to walk away from him again.

CHAPTER ELEVEN

"Please, Marti. I love you. Don't go."

She closed her eyes and set her hand on the knob.

"If you walk out of here, I'm going with you, and I won't leave your side. I'll move in with you and drive you crazy until you start to trust me and realize I'm nothing like Mike!"

Marti gave a sarcastic laugh. "You couldn't move in with me. You hate my apartment. It's too *cozy!*"

"What do you do?" Doug returned. "Write down every word I say and figure out how to use it against me? Do you enjoy making me crazy?"

"You're making *me* crazy!" she shouted.

He held up his hands in challenge and forced his voice to a more reasonable level. "I have something to say, and I intend to say it."

"Whether I want to hear it or not?"

"Yes!"

Marti stared at him for a moment, then swiveled on her heel and stalked to the couch. "I'm listening," she said in a tone that said she couldn't care less what he had to say.

"First take your coat off."

"Why?"

"Take your damned coat off!" he bellowed.

Marti jerked off her coat and flung it on a chair with furious impact.

Breathless from the exchange, Doug raked both hands through his hair. "Trish and I go to Los Angeles every year for a big convention for the recording industry," he said. "It's called the National Association of Music Merchandisers. Trish goes to promote her albums, just as hundreds of other musicians do. I go for business reasons. And, contrary to what she wanted you to think, we don't stay together."

"But you had such *fun* last year!" Marti reminded him caustically.

"Yeah," he agreed. "With about ten others who hung out together. We did have a good time. And I hardly saw her the whole time. She's playing a game with you, Marti. Don't fall for it."

Marti wanted to believe, but anger and fresh hurt still reigned. "Then why do you? Why do you stand there and let her put her hands all over you? Why do you listen when she says those things?"

He heaved a weary sigh and pulled out a cigarette, contemplating it as if it held life's secrets. "Because I know the fear that's behind it all. I know why she's doing it. It's like she's grasping for a lifeline."

"And you're it?" She stood up and paced across the room, then turned back to him. "Doug, how do you think I feel hearing the two of you talking about being in L.A. together when I'm so unsophisticated that I've never even been there? Breckenridge was supposed to be my big adventure! It meant independence, control. . . ." She clutched her forehead, then threw up her hands and uttered a mirthless laugh. "What a joke!

160

And I have to stand there and measure myself against her, knowing that she's still in love with you—"

"She's not!"

"Yes, she is. I can tell."

"You just don't know her," he said. "She can't love. All she can do is need. She thinks she needs me more than anyone else, so she's possessive of me. Love is not the same thing as need, Marti!"

"Just look at her!" Marti shouted. "She slinks in in her tight leather skirt and her low-cut cashmere sweater, with an emerald on her neck! An emerald, Doug, and I don't even own jade!"

"I'll buy you an emerald if you want one. Or jade or whatever the hell—"

"You don't understand!" she shouted. "She drops her sable coat to the ground like it's last year's contribution to the Salvation Army! And I'm standing there in a faded pair of three-year-old jeans and an old bulky sweater." Her eyes bubbled over with tears, and she slapped them away. "And then she sashays back out to get into her gold Jaguar that's parked next to your Porsche!"

"What do you have against my Porsche, for God's sake?"

"Nothing!" she shouted. "It's just that I realize that we're from two different worlds. You see me as a challenge now—a pretty, new challenge that needed you for a while. But what about when I'm not hurting? Mike was intrigued with the newness, too, for a while. The novelty of a woman outside his class, but he couldn't seem to stop drifting back to the women who slept in diamonds and silk and bathed in Parisian perfume. It'll be the same with you. What about when I stop needing you and I only love you, and you see that I'm just a farmer's daughter with no distinguishing traits. I'm not famous, I'm not rich—"

"Back up," he said, his eyes brightening and clinging to the subconscious message. "You said you loved me."

"No, I didn't." Her face went white. Had she?

"Yes, you did. You said when you stop needing me and you only love me. Do you love me now?"

"You aren't listening to me!" she said. Her hands were trembling, and she forced herself to stay out of his reach.

"Yes, I am! You aren't listening to *yourself.* You just said you loved me!"

"LOOK AT ME!" she shouted desperately, gritting out the words. "I can't love you. I'm nobody."

"You *can* love me!" He was smiling now, and stepping nearer to her, and she knew that if he touched her she would dissolve into a heap of dust. "You can even marry me."

Her gasp sent her into a fit of coughing, during which she choked out an astonished, "What?"

"Are you listening, Marti?" He reached her then and drew her into his arms as she recovered, and she was powerless to push him away. "I'm asking you to marry me. Because you are somebody. You're the only woman who's ever pushed me to near insanity. And knowing you has made me richer than money ever did." His lips touched her forehead, and he began trailing tiny kisses down her temple. "Be my wife. Have my children. Need me. Love me."

"You don't know what you're saying," she cried against him. "You're . . . you're . . ."

"I'm intoxicated," he explained against her cheek. "I made love to you tonight, remember?" When she looked up at him and touched his face, as if by touching she could *feel* if he meant what he said, he whispered, "And I fell in love with you the first night I met you."

It couldn't be true. Love didn't come that easily, that unconditionally, did it? She hadn't earned it, hadn't deserved it, hadn't even asked for it. And yet he was offering it to her.

"So will you marry me?"

She smiled. "No."

His face fell. "Why?"

She didn't know why. "Because." She dropped a kiss on his neck.

"I'll keep at you until you do, you know."

"I know." She opened the shirt he had pulled on and left unbuttoned in his haste to leave.

"We'll talk about marriage tomorrow," he whispered. "Tonight I'll settle for just being loved and cherished."

Marti looked up into his warm, honest eyes, and she saw that he was serious.

Serious . . . about being in love with her since the night of her concussion.

Serious . . . about moving lock, stock, and barrel into her life.

Serious . . . about making her his wife.

His mustache tickled her neck when he dipped his head to nuzzle her throat, and a shiver scampered across the surface of her skin.

He nuzzled the side of her neck and buried his lips in a strand of hair caught on her shoulder. "God, your hair is so soft," he whispered. "It smells like sunset, and feels like a summer breeze." He lifted his face and took a handful of it, breathed it in. "And at night I dream about it sweeping across my face . . . and my mouth, and my chest. . . ."

She took his face in her hands and kissed him. The kiss bloomed and colored with the depth of a rose, swirling with the power of a jealous wind, drawing from her a sureness of life, of love, a sureness no longer bred in fantasy. It was the shattering, sharp sense of reality. Reality that could make or break a heart. Reality that forced decision. And the decision was hers.

She let him back her to the couch, and stood on her toes to deepen their kiss. And as his hands slid up her sides, under her sweater, the decision was made. Somehow there was a purpose being fulfilled here, and she wasn't going to fight it anymore.

"I love you," he whispered again. "I love you . . . I love you . . ."

Though she could not yet utter the words herself, she could have listened to him say them a million times, in as many ways, for the glittering ardor in his eyes multiplied with each pronouncement. He could have loved her over and over for three lifetimes, and still it would not have been enough.

Marti slowed her car as she approached Trish Tanner's mountain hideaway, nestled in the mountainside as if it were a part of nature itself. Over the week that had passed since Doug told her he loved her, Marti felt herself surrendering to the love she had once so feared because of Trish Tanner. She took a deep breath and reminded herself that this meeting was an investment in her future. Her future with Doug.

She shivered as she remembered the call she'd made from work this morning after she'd talked Reed, Doug's assistant, into giving her Trish's number—so she could try to make friends with her, she'd told him. But there would never be any friendship between the two women. That had been apparent from the moment Marti had identified herself on the phone.

"What do you want?" Trish had asked in her husky, undaunted voice.

"I want to talk to you about Doug," Marti said without fanfare. "He's obviously important to both of us, and I think we should come to some sort of agreement."

"I'm listening." Was there a note of amusement in Trish's voice?

"Not on the phone," Marti said. "I want to talk in person."

Had she been crazy? she wondered now, swallowing back her feeling of intimidation as she approached the round vacation home on the bluff. What did she hope to accomplish by coming here to Trish's turf? A truce? An understanding that Marti meant to stay in Doug's life? A threat that she wanted Trish out of his life? Of course not. Obviously, Trish meant something to him. He was her friend, and he cared for her. Marti had no intention of taking that away from him. She only wanted Trish to understand where she fit in.

She pulled her Mazda up into the winding driveway and cut off the engine, though the motor continued to spit and whine for a few seconds longer. Her eyes drifted to the Jaguar parked outside a three-car ga-

165

rage, and suddenly she felt mousy and miserable again.

She got out of the car and straightened her fake-fur coat and thought about the sable Trish had so idly thrown over her shoulder last night. It didn't matter, she told herself. Doug wanted her the way she was. He fell in love with her when she was wearing bruises and bandages. No emeralds, no furs, no glamor. Just Marti.

If she could only remember that, she thought.

She rang the bell and waited a few moments. The door opened, and she braced herself.

Trish leaned against the jamb, a yellow silk Japanese kimono draped over her tall body, her hair draped over her shoulders, and her arms folded tightly over her waist. "Come in," Trish said. "I honestly didn't think you'd have the nerve to follow through with this."

Marti straightened her already-stiff posture and faced her in the foyer. "Why not? I can be as determined as you when I want something."

Trish tipped back her head and assessed her with serious hazel eyes. "Yes, I can see that." Pursing her lips, she led Marti into a living room with shiny hardwood floors and glass panels that held a panoramic view of the Rockies. "Poor Doug," Trish said on a sigh. "Always a sucker for a blonde."

Marti couldn't help smiling at the barb. Were they already launching their battle? She declined Trish's offer of a chair and looked around the room. Dark, oriental sculpture decorated the green tables, and even the beams that crossed the room overhead were strategically accented with small pieces of art. Against one wall stood a three-foot black marble panther hunched as if ready to pounce. A grand piano filled one area of the large room next to the wall that held a montage of Trish Tanner memorabilia—from photos in national magazines to snapshots taken by friends. Framed at the center of the photos was an eight-by-ten of Trish enfolded in Doug's embrace, obviously taken years ago, but reinforcing the complicated relationship in Marti's mind. On the outer fringe of the photos was one of a little hollow-eyed girl standing between her parents, parents who must have been snatched away shortly after the picture was taken, according to Doug's account. A sudden rush of sympathy ambushed Marti, and she took a deep, futile breath and moved her eyes back to the frosty woman who was waiting for her to make the next move. Who was she dealing with? The panther or the abandoned child?

"I realize that you and Doug are very close friends," she began, "and I have no intention of standing in the way of that—"

Trish laughed aloud, but the sound held a shrill echo of desperation. "Well, considering that you have no other choice, that's rather big of you."

Marti leveled her cool eyes on the woman and went on. "I also realize that you and I will never be friends, and that's fine with me."

Trish snickered and crossed her arms.

"But I wanted to make it clear to you that I'm in love with Doug and I don't plan to step aside for you or anyone else."

Trish's grin faded slowly. She went to her mantel, opened a gold-plated box, and took out a cigarette. "I almost feel sorry for you," Trish whispered.

Marti watched, nonplussed, as Trish lit the Virginia Slim with great aplomb, then blew a stream of smoke, her cloud of threat and wisdom, toward Marti. "Do you know I was the first woman who ever meant anything to him? Do you know that I was the first woman he ever made love to? Did he tell you that?"

Marti swallowed. "He told me that it's been over for years."

Trish issued a quiet laugh and leaned over the table. "Don't you realize it can never be over? We were everything to each other. We saved each other from our pasts, and our pains, and our stifling little worlds. We made each other. And all these years we've been there for one another. I haven't met a woman yet who could come between us—really come between us—and better women than you have tried."

Marti felt the tenuous grips of her confidence slipping, but she refused to let it show on her face. It wasn't new, this knowledge that they meant so much to each other, and she had decided to accept it.

"Do you realize what kind of women have made plays for Doug?" Trish went on. "Princesses, and movie stars, and I can't even count all the musicians. Wealthy women, talented women, women who had everything, much more than you have with your big, wounded eyes and your pouting lips and the hair that *might* make men look twice but grows boring after a while. He grew tired of the others. He'll grow tired of you."

Pain slashed across Marti's eyes, across her heart, but she refused to be defeated. "Did he ask the others to marry him? Did he ask you?"

The flicker of surprise that crossed over Trish's features suddenly recharged the failing certainty in Marti's mind, and instantly she was aware that she had the real strength in this room, and that the tight bravado in Trish's attitude was only a facade for terror.

She looked away for a few seconds, then said, "Doug doesn't believe in marriage."

"Wrong," Marti returned. "He asked me to marry him just last week."

Before Marti's eyes, Trish's face went pale. Inhaling her cigarette, she turned back to Marti. "Doug always has been a passionate man. He often doesn't even remember what he's said in the heat of that passion."

Trish's effort to convince her it meant nothing only served to make Marti more certain Doug's proposal had been genuine and unique. "We weren't making love when he asked me. And he's asked several times since."

Trish only stared at her, her translucent skin beginning to pinken as a desperate wildness sparked in her eyes. "Well, that leaves you with a choice, then, doesn't it?" She inhaled the cigarette, trembling in her fingers, and narrowed her eyes as she released the smoke. "You can marry him or you can get out of his life once and for all."

"Why would I want to do that?" Marti asked with disbelief.

"Because if you don't," Trish said distinctly, "I'll ruin him."

Marti felt panic rising inside her, but she controlled it. "You wouldn't do that to him. You couldn't."

Trish's face was expressionless. "Try me." She stepped toward Marti. "Have you ever heard of piracy?" she asked between her teeth. "Like when someone illegally reproduces recordings and sells them without reporting the sales and without paying the artist royalties? It's done a lot, and it's something that musicians are pretty paranoid about."

"So?"

"So if it were to get out that Duziak Productions were pirating the recordings made there, how many musicians do you think would want to use his studio?"

Marti didn't answer. She simply stared at the woman before her, astonished. It didn't matter that she could see and feel Trish's fear, and knew that behind the cold exterior was stark panic that would have made her use anything to get her way.

"He'd be ruined in a week," Trish said.

"You couldn't prove it because it isn't true."

The sparkle returned to Trish's eyes. "I wouldn't have to. The very suggestion coming from me—someone so close to Doug—would be enough. Even if people didn't really believe it, there would be that slightest seed of doubt in their minds. No one would take the chance. The studio is everything to Doug. Take it away from him and see what's left. I dare you."

Marti's eyes stung with the threat of tears. "You would hurt him that way, when you claim to care for him?"

"Only if I have to," Trish said.

Marti felt paralyzed, frozen where she stood, as a million possibilities shot through her mind. *The studio is my life,* he'd told her once. And Trish had the power to destroy it.

"The choice is yours," Trish said. "Marry him and ruin him, or leave him and save him."

"What are you afraid of?" Marti asked suddenly.

170

"What is it about me that frightens you so? Is it that Doug loves me? That he won't be there for you to cling to if he's with me? Is that it?"

Trish hardened her features and looked at the woman she had made her enemy. "Get out," she said quietly. "All the way out."

Marti drew in a deep, despairing breath and walked toward the door, pitying the woman more than she pitied herself for the decision she would have to make. Before she opened it, she turned back to Trish.

"I'll leave him," Marti said in a cracked voice, "to keep you from destroying him. But if you ever hurt him, so help me God, I'll be back. And you'll be sorry."

And then Marti left her to do the hardest thing she'd ever done in her life.

CHAPTER TWELVE

"I'm going back to Florida," Marti told Doug that night, standing frigidly with her eyes focused on the table between them.

"You're what?" The hurt in his voice cut through her cool facade and made her want to change her mind. But she couldn't, not if she loved him. For she had no doubt in her mind that Trish had the power to break him. And if she did, it would take more than love to put him back together.

"I'm leaving. I'm going back for good."

He stood up, his face pale with denial. "But . . . what about us? You can't just walk out!"

She stiffened her shoulders and forced herself to look into those warm, soothing eyes, those eyes that had come to mean so much more than security to her. The words stumbled from her lips like self-ruinous weapons. "It's . . . Mike. I've decided to try it again with him. He wants me back, and he seems sincere—"

Doug knocked his chair over with the force of his wrath, and bent over the table to her. "You're leaving me to go back to a man who cheated on you?"

She swallowed the lump in her throat and nodded. "Yes. I tried to get over him. But I couldn't."

Doug moved quickly around the table, grabbed her chin, and forced her to look at him fully. "Look at me! You made love to me. I was your first! Don't tell me you still loved him when you were making love to me, because I won't believe you!"

Her eyes filled with anguish, and she breathed in a sob and touched his face, the face that would be indelibly etched on her memory for the rest of her life, the face of the man who had saved her, who had comforted her, who had loved her. . . . "I'm so sorry," she whispered. "I don't want to hurt you."

She saw the despair in his eyes, and the astonished, broken expression on his face, and it twisted her soul. He dropped his fist to the table, stared down at it. "Why are you so afraid of loving me, Marti? If it's still my money . . ."

"It's not your money," she managed to say. "It's just that Mike and I need to try to work things out."

He looked up at her, his limpid green eyes refusing to believe her shallow words. "He can't love you, Marti. Not like I can. No one can love you like I can."

Tears clung like crystal to the tips of her lashes. "You're special, Doug. I won't forget you."

A lightning current of anger whipped across his eyes. "Well, that's just real consoling," he muttered sardonically. "When you made me think you cared was it some sadistic power game just to see how I'd react? Was it another of your little advance and retreat games? An exercise in control?"

She closed her eyes. "Doug, don't."

"Why, Marti?" he asked, his own eyes shimmering with moist agony. "Why did you make love with me? Why did you let me be the first? Why did you teach me to feel again? Numbness is a helluva lot better than this. Why, Marti?"

Any words she could have uttered in answer were stillborn, like the joy that had been aborted with Trish's threat.

"Tell me why, damn it!" Doug shouted.

She jumped at the force of his demand, and covered her face as tears leapt over her lashes. "I don't know," she cried.

The tears she struggled with softened his fury, and he sat back down and stared at his fists coiled on the table. "You don't know," he repeated with despair. "You don't know."

An infinite chasm of silence yawned between them, and finally Doug looked up at her. "When . . . when are you going?"

"A few days. When I can get things at work tied up. I can't just leave them flat, but I have to go."

"Marti, please . . . don't leave me." The plea was not an easy one, and it came out as a defeated sigh. He looked around at the small apartment. How could he make her understand? "I had so many plans. You finally made things bright for me." He reached out for her hand, stopping just short of touching her. "And I did for you. I know I did."

She withdrew her hand so he couldn't touch her, for if he did . . . "Yes, you did," she said, wiping her face. "And I'm thankful for that. But it doesn't change things."

He stared at her for a stricken moment, all the pain in his life compressed in the misty green of his eyes, and she yearned to hold him and comfort him, the way he had done with her.

"All this time that you were worried about competing with Trish, I had no idea I'd wind up competing with some jerk I've never even seen. Some fool who doesn't even know how precious you are. Some bastard who doesn't understand how priceless your love can be."

He snatched up his duffel bag, lying on the couch where he'd left it when he spent the night last night, and went into the bedroom for the rest of his things. When he came back out he looked at her as if he would awake from this nightmare any moment and find that she still loved him. "He doesn't deserve you, Marti," he said. "And you don't deserve him."

Before she had to dredge up the strength for another lie, he left her without looking back. And as much as Marti wanted to go after him, she loved him enough to let him go.

She lay in bed that night staring up at the ceiling. Her pillow was wet beneath her head, and her hair was soaked from absorbing the tears that had flowed ceaselessly all night long. What would she do now? What on earth would she do now?

And what would Doug do, and think, and feel? Was she leaving him to be devoured by the wolf side of Trish Tanner? When all along it was the other side, the little girl afraid of being alone, dictating their lives.

It was best, she told herself. He'd spent a lifetime building a career, and surely if the choice were his, he'd prefer losing her than losing it. It was the source of his wealth, more basic to him than love could ever be. She wouldn't force him to make that decision. Besides, she thought miserably, Trish had given her the choice. Not him.

The martyr role felt lousy, she thought as she pulled out of bed and looked out her window. Flurries of snow blew against the glass like plastic crumbs in a paperweight, and the cars lining the parking lot looked as if they had been tucked in for the night with velvet-white blankets.

A lone stroller in a dark leather bomber jacket scuffed through the snow, a lit cigarette in his mouth. Her heart leapt, then crashed. It was Doug, walking through the snow outside her apartment, sorting through his own dejection and trying to make some sense of it all.

"Oh, God, don't let him love me," she prayed, moving from the window and going back to bed as new tears pressed out of her eyes. "Don't let him hurt."

But as clearly as if she were him, she felt the piercing pain and the empty bewilderment of the man outside her window, standing in the cold as if he'd just lost his best friend. His lover. His life.

In the parking lot, Doug leaned against a car and dusted off some of the snow with a gloved hand. The slopes would be great tomorrow, he thought. He would have loved to take Marti over to Keystone and make first tracks with her. He would have loved to be the one to teach her the right way to ski.

But Marti didn't like to take chances after she'd had time to think, he told himself. Her fear of the mountain was deep-seated, just as her fear of love was. Maybe that was why she'd decided to take another chance on Mike. Maybe she figured it was better to take a risk on something you already knew. Doug had loved her unconditionally, and she had not known how to accept that. Maybe that was his mistake.

But how else did a man love a woman?

He kicked the snow at his feet and dropped his cigarette, stamped it out. The temperature was dropping further, and he shivered against it. He didn't know why he was surprised, really. For a while he had thought that God had dropped her into his path, so that for once in his life he could love someone who loved him in return, not for what he could give them, but for what he was. And for that he had wanted to give her everything. *Everything.*

But it wasn't that way. Instead, she had just been another reminder that he was destined to be alone for the rest of his life. His eyes misted over and he looked up at the stars, so scattered and numbered and oblique against the black backdrop of the heavens. *Why?* he asked furiously. *Why?*

But no answer came.

Marti spent a mechanical day at work the next day. Then she came home and wept until she was empty. Occasionally that night her mind would grasp for ways to talk Trish out of this ultimatum by appealing to her sense of friendship for Doug. But she knew Trish was going to see that her own needs were filled no matter how it hurt Doug.

She could scratch her eyes out or grovel on hands and knees. But that wasn't her style, and she knew it wouldn't work. It would only be playing the game Trish's way, and the woman was an expert at both those ploys. She could never win. Never.

The phone rang, and she grabbed a Kleenex and

blew her nose before she answered it. "Hello?" she said, tentatively.

"It's Amanda," her friend said, the background noise of the Pegasus making it difficult to hear. "I'm at work. I wanted to tell you that Doug's here. It's breaking my heart. He's sitting over by himself in the corner, staring at his drink. He's exhausted and he looks terrible. He needs you, Marti. Can't you come?"

Marti closed her eyes to squeeze back her fresh surge of tears. Where did they keep coming from? she wondered as she struggled for an answer. She had told Amanda the same thing she told Doug. That she was leaving him for Mike. "No, Amanda. There's no point."

Amanda groaned. "All right, but if you ask me, you're an idiot. Anybody can see that Doug's better for you than Mike. How much evidence do you need before you realize it?"

"Thanks for calling, Amanda," she said, choking back a sob. "You'd better get back to work."

She hung up the phone and Amanda's words rang in her ears. She didn't need any evidence to see how special he was. It was Trish who needed the evidence. Trish who . . .

A light suddenly dawned in her mind, and she slid her hands down her face and sat erect. *Evidence!* Doug had the evidence that he had written her songs. Evidence that could parry Trish's attempts to ruin him. Evidence that could do Trish much more damage than she could do him.

Springing up, she laughed aloud. She didn't have to leave Doug! He had taken care of himself years ago, when he decided to hang on to the proof that he'd written those songs. He must have known. He must have known!

She ran to her closet and pulled out her coat, and laughed again as relief overwhelmed her. Thank God neither of them would have to hurt anymore.

The thundering sound of applause penetrated Doug's thoughts as the entertainers Marti had booked for the Pegasus ended a song and started another.

The void within him, too large to be numbed by the liquor, grew to encompass the room. The thought of his loss coiled inside him until he wanted to crawl all the way inside himself. The song called to a lover who was not there, mourning the hours alone, recalling her touch. And that he could relate to.

If he could just have another chance to make her love him. If he could just make love to her one more time, drawing out the aftermath until morning and on into the next day, merging days and nights into eternity before she had the time to slip away again. God, how he missed her. What would the pain be like a year from now? Five years from now?

Opening his eyes, he panned the audience, the faces turned up to the stage in true reaction to the song, faces quiet, faces smiling, faces . . .

His thoughts trailed off when a very special face at the entrance of the smoky lounge caught his eye and his breath and his heart.

Marti's face.

Their eyes locked across the distance that seemed like miles, across the sea of people, across the loss and harsh words and problems and past that seemed magnified when they came together. Had she come to see

179

Amanda, who was scurrying from table to table delivering drinks, or had she come to see him? His heart hammered against his chest, his fingers on his glass seemed suddenly cold and clammy, and the deepest part of him responded at the sight of her. Her hair, a wavy, shimmering veil around her breasts, seemed even blonder tonight than he remembered. The powder-blue blouse she wore was open at the neck, revealing the faintest hint of cleavage. She smiled as their eyes met, telling him the anguish was over, looking at him with eyes the color of promise.

It was as though they were alone in an empty room, and both their pasts dissolved like dust in the wind. Either she was his for life or she was giving him one more chance. She had had second thoughts or she had discarded those hindering thoughts altogether. She would love him tonight or loving would never have meaning for him again. He stood up and walked toward her.

Her heart bolted as he came nearer, the low roar of people enjoying the evening fading in and out like background noise in a dream.

His loden eyes were brilliant against the yellow glow of candlelight, smoky green as a sunset sea, drowning her in their depths as they had when he'd made love to her. Taking a deep, shuddering breath, she felt the chasm of pain and injustice shrinking between them. She swallowed, anticipating the first words, foolishly wondering what she would say.

But apprehension was swept away when he took her face with his hands. His kiss was as unexpected as it was welcome, and her heart groped for a beat, her lungs pressed for air against her chest, and her body strove for closer, more fulfilling contact. His tongue tasted, turned, moved against hers in slow, sensual rhythm as an explosive sigh shivered in a moan from his throat. His hands buried themselves in her hair, molding over her scalp with unwielding pressure until the moment he freed her. But she was not free when they were separate. "I love you, Doug," she whispered, her voice hoarse, breathy, ragged. "I can't help loving you."

The admission caused a lump to lodge in his throat, and he swallowed it back. As if he couldn't believe she was more than a dream, he touched her face with gentle fingers that begged her not to turn away again.

She turned her lips to caress his warm knuckles. His hand turned over against her mouth, and she took it and pressed a kiss into his palm. "Let's go home," she whispered.

"Mine or yours?" he asked softly.

"It doesn't matter," she said. "Home is not a place."

"No," he agreed. "It's not."

The stillness of the cold night when he whisked her out serenaded them, and his arms were around her in the darkness, his body tight against hers, the steam of his breath warming her face.

His lips descended on hers, and this time his tongue ravished, plundered, stirred her senses to raw peaks. Without breaking the kiss, he took the coat hanging limply in her hand and pulled it around her shoulders, clutching the edges roughly to pull her more securely against him until her soft breasts crushed into his chest. One hand left the coat and slid beneath it, found the bottom of her blouse and eased under it.

Losing her balance, she stepped back, but he met her with a step forward, supporting her against the brick wall of the lodge. His hand began its journey up the bare flesh of her back, and Marti drew his waist against her, pulling his sweater out of his jeans and making contact with his flesh. His growing arousal hungered her into quivering impatience. She left his back and traced the tight planes of his buttocks, driving her own hips hard against him to relieve some of the throbbing in her core, but the contact only heightened her need.

"I could take you right here," he groaned against her ear, his breath coming in shivers. "Since yesterday all I've thought of was the way you smell, the way you smile, the way your body feels next to mine . . ."

"Me, too," she whispered.

His hands slipped into the waistband of her jeans, kneading the soft curves, moving her against him in a sensual rhythm while his tongue thrust against hers. Voices upwind startled them, and with one quick, shallow breath, he pulled back, breaking all contact with her, and raked a rough hand through his hair.

Feeling as if she'd been awakened from a dream and found herself cold and alone, Marti reached for him. "We'd better go," she suggested softly.

"Yeah," he said, and looked down the dark hill leading to their condominiums, mentally measuring the distance. Then, with a frustrated glance back at her, he muttered, "Damn!" swept her up in his arms, and started walking.

Marti snuggled against his neck. "I love you, Doug."

"I love you, Hot Dog," he whispered, but his words faded out as he slowed his steps and kissed her again.

They were barely inside the door when he set her down, his hand sliding up the curves of her body as she straightened before him. As if it had been an eternity since the last kiss, they came together impatiently, silky tongues twining as a prelude to the union that would follow.

His body was warm, despite the chilling wind that had followed them home, and he smelled of fresh mountain air. His chest heaved beneath her touch, and she fumbled with his shirt, freeing buttons and burying her hands in the crisp hair of his chest, finding the straining granules of his male nipples and feathering her fingernails across them, his deep, low moan making her body ripen for his.

"I love you," she whispered.

"Say it again," he said, his eyes so intent that she felt them molding her soul.

She slid open his shirt, trailing kisses across his chest. "I love you. I love you. I love you." Her lips traveled lower as she pulled his shirt from his pants. His stomach was hard and smooth against her mouth, inspiring warmth and fire that balled inside her and fell to a region where arousal was beginning to take life. Sliding her hands up his ribs, she pulled the shirt farther back, then pushed it off his shoulders, freeing his arms. His hands came immediately back to her.

"You are so beautiful," she whispered, running her hands down his chest and brushing through the sprinkle of hair that caught seductively at the base of her fingers. "Such a beautiful man."

His fingers tangled in the roots of her hair, and she

felt the tremor of restraint shiver through him as her hands went lower, tracing the line of his jeans as he moaned and pulled her closer. He wanted to hold her until next year, wanted to kiss her forever, wanted to stretch the moment into infinity.

She felt him lowering to the floor, pulling her with him, shifting her hips above his until his arousal warmed the center of her own heat. The kiss was plundering, and his bare chest pressed against her breasts. His hands moving across her back slid the sweater up.

Breaking free of his lips, Marti pushed his shoulders until she sat up on him, still weighted against the hard reminder of their urgency. She slid off her sweater. His hands were anxious, his eyes were hooded, and when her breasts were fully exposed, round and taut and straining almost painfully for his touch, she threw the sweater aside. "The first day I met you," she said in a breathy, hoarse voice, "I wanted to make love to you when I was supposed to be grieving over Mike."

His hands moved to her breasts, and she arched against them, offering everything as he partook slowly. He tried to raise up, but she pushed him back down, bending over him as he began to move eloquently beneath her. Her mouth sought his nipples, drawing shivers and tremors with each nip of her teeth.

Raising slightly, she slipped her hands beneath her and touched him intimately through his clothes, feeling the denim stretched without relief over explosive desire. Unclasping his pants, she pulled the zipper down and began a slow, sensuous massage.

"You're driving me crazy," he said in a tremulous voice, trying to raise up again. This time when she tried to push him back, he pulled her down against him, kissing her with the fury and frustration of the hours he had suffered without her. His hands roved down her soft back, then slid beneath her pants to touch soft, bare flesh. His ministrations made her shiver and moan against him.

"I can't stand it," she gasped against his ear, and he turned her on her back, peeled the pants off her long legs, and then stepped out of his own. He lowered his mouth to one luscious, throbbing breast, wet it with his tongue, circled, bit, and pulled, thrilling at the desire rushing through her in the form of a quiver, and the sound of her moans as her fingers tangled in his hair. One of her knees rose, and her back arched upward as he suckled. He thought she was more beautiful at that moment than any woman he'd ever seen.

Finally he moved her legs and entered her, showing her with his body that this union surpassed anything that had come before.

With one deep thrust, he raised up to look at her, memorizing the look of bliss-filled desire on her face, in case it should be once more snatched from him. Moving inside her again, he went deeper, and she clutched at his shoulders, begging for more depth and more speed. But he would not be hurried. "I love you, Marti," he whispered, his breath a shudder against her lips. "I wish I could make love to you all day. I don't want it to be over. I don't want to let you go." With another shift of his hips, he thrust again, making her whimper against his shoulder.

Sliding her hands down his back, she pressed against his buttocks. His body was covered with sweat as he let go and followed the rhythm that took control of their hearts and lungs and minds and bodies, until finally they both soared past the stars, breathless, ecstatic, mindless, hot, sated, loved until a million tiny explosions set off within them both.

Afterward, they lay clinging to each other, neither willing to break the spell with words. Marti thought her heart would burst with love for him, love so strong that it erased the shadows of her life and pointed her toward the future. She looked at him, at the thoughts evident in his glazed eyes, at the tight set of his lips, and wondered why he looked so sad when she felt as if joy had been packaged and offered to her.

Would she abandon him again? he wondered with despair. Would he be able to make her stay? Would he ever trust the happiness they gave to each other, the happiness that was as fleeting as the night itself? Or would it be gone as quickly as it had come? "Are you still going home to Florida?" he asked cautiously.

"Of course not," she whispered, lifting her face to look at him more fully. "I love you."

He swallowed. "I thought you loved me before, but you were going back to him."

She dropped a kiss in the indentation below his throat. "No, I wasn't. It was the only excuse I could think of."

"Excuse?" He pulled her up and glared into her eyes. "Why'd you need an excuse to leave me?"

She dropped her head, letting her hair form a veil over her face. "Because . . . it seemed like the right thing—"

"The right thing? To tear me apart?"

"I had to. Trish said—" She cut off her words, realizing that it would serve no purpose to let him know how Trish had manipulated her, and how little his friendship with the woman really meant.

"Trish said what? What did she say, Marti?"

Marti shook her head and pulled from his embrace. "Nothing. It's over now. I'm not leaving you again."

He sat up, his face glowering. "It isn't over. Trish had something to do with this, didn't she?"

"Doug, it doesn't matter."

"The hell it doesn't!" he shouted, startling her. "Get dressed, Marti. We're going to see Trish."

"Now?"

"Damn right."

"But—"

"Get dressed!" he ordered again, and swallowing back her retort, she did as he said.

Hardly a word was spoken on the ride over to Trish's house. His anger was volcanic, but his hand clutching hers tightly told Marti it was not directed at her.

When they reached Trish's house he pulled Marti behind him to the door and banged furiously on it. And when Trish opened it he burst in without a word of greeting.

"Doug!" Trish gasped. "What . . . what is it?" She gave Marti a worried glance.

Somehow the woman standing before Marti, with fear and apprehension in her eyes, didn't look quite as intimidating, or quite as glamorous as she had before. She was just a woman, one who had lost at her own game, one who, of her own accord, had cut her only lifeline. "I changed my mind, Trish."

Trish's hazel eyes flickered with challenge. "You could always change it again."

Marti squeezed Doug's hand. "I'm here to stay."

Trish's nostrils flared the slightest bit, and she looked helplessly at Doug. Then she drew her gaze back to Marti and stiffened her lips. "I don't bluff, you know. I mean everything I say."

"What are you talking about, Trish?" Doug demanded through his teeth.

Trish averted her eyes and went to her mantel for a cigarette. "It's between Marti and me," she said quietly.

Doug looked from one to the other. "No. This is about me. This has something to do with why Marti came home yesterday and broke things off with me, and you're going to tell me now."

The two women's eyes locked in silent battle, and neither answered.

"Now, Trish!" he shouted.

Tears filled Trish's eyes, and she turned to Doug with all the dramatics of a daytime drama star. "It's only because you mean so much to me, Doug," she whispered. "And I need you."

"What did you say to her?" Doug asked, no longer affected by Trish's theatrics. "Just tell me what you said."

Trish started toward him, but he shook her off. "I knew that if she were in the way, you'd never be there for me. And I'm so desperate! My career is on the line."

"What did you say to her?" he asked again, snipping out each word.

Trish wiped at her tears and stiffened. "I said that I would start a rumor that you had been pirating if she didn't get out of your life." She swallowed and lifted her eyes to Doug's. "I meant it, Doug. I'll do it if you don't help me."

Doug looked at Marti with eyes that contained a million emotions. "That was why?" he whispered, suddenly smiling. "That was why you said you were going back to Mike? For me? How many times do I have to tell you how important you are to me? My studio is nothing to me anymore compared to what I feel for you."

She focused on the buttons of his shirt and tried not to cry as he gathered her against him.

"Don't you know she can't hurt me?" he whispered, as if he'd forgotten Trish was there. "Don't you realize that's why I kept the songs locked away all these years?"

Marti looked up at him. "I realized it tonight. That you have leverage. That's why I came back to you."

"What?" Trish's question swam on a shaky wave of panic. "What leverage? What are you talking about?"

Doug turned back to her, as if he didn't even need to honor her with an explanation. "The songs, Trish. I have every version of the songs, from the very first. Evidence that I wrote them. Evidence that you're a fraud. At least that's how the press would see it, after all your hoopla about how they came to you, and what inspired them, and how you've been able to develop as a writer. It's all a crock, isn't it, Trish? How would you feel if suddenly everybody knew?"

Trish shook her head, her eyes luminous with despondency. "You . . . you wouldn't do that."

"Not unless it was the only way to defend myself, and Marti, and my studio against your bitter, petty manipulations. Not unless you pushed me far enough."

Like a devastated child, she covered her contorted face with trembling hands. "Doug, how could you? Why did you save them?"

"Because I know you, Trish. I know how you work, and how you think. And I knew that someday I might have to use them to protect myself from you. You can't just be a friend, can you? You have to use, and control, and manipulate. I just wanted to be your friend, Trish. But that wasn't enough, was it?"

"But you've *always* been there, Doug!"

"Not anymore I won't. I'm tired of your games and your lies. And I'm tired of your little power plays. Find someone else to cling to with those claws of yours. Get out of my life."

Trish looked very tired suddenly, and very small, and once again Marti pitied her. *I was one of the only people who ever cared what happened to her,* Doug had said once. And now Trish had destroyed even that. As Doug began pulling Marti toward the door, Trish's forlorn expression touched her, and Marti reached out to her.

Trish's eyes brimmed with tears as they locked coldly on Marti.

"I'm going to marry Doug," Marti told her softly. "But I don't want to take him from you to do it. If you want to be Doug's friend, just his friend, I won't stand between you. But if you try to come between us again, you'll regret that you ever saw my face. I understand you more than you realize, and I don't blame you for fighting. But that doesn't excuse any of it."

Trish's mouth twitched, and covering it with one

hand, she opened the door with the other. When they were outside she slammed it behind them.

"You'll really marry me?" Doug whispered in the night air.

"Yes." His arms tightened around her, and she closed her eyes. "I love you, Doug. And I'll never leave you again."

"You won't have the chance," he promised. "Because I'm not letting you out of my sight. You're stuck with me, Hot Dog."

Marti Jackson felt the majestic feeling of joy as she whisked behind Doug down the steep Breckenridge slopes a week later. He had taught her control over her skis and abandonment over her emotions. He had taught her the ecstasy of love and trust. He had taught her that his money and his studio were no more than added spice on the life they would build together, and now she wasn't afraid.

He stopped at the bottom of Silverthorn and waited for her, and she skied to a halt beside him, smiling victoriously up into his mirrored glasses. *My escort to the altar,* she thought when he wrapped an arm around her. And heaven was a white-powdered slope on a conquered mountain, and the trusting arms of the man she loved.